BRAGAN UNIVERSITY SERIES
BOOK ONE

BETTER WITH YOU

GIANNA GABRIELA

Better With You
Bragan University Series (Book One)

ISBN: 9781981439577

Cover design, editing, & formatting by Lauren Dawes (Sly Fox Cover Designs).

DEDICATION

To Lauren, because without you this book wouldn't be what it is. You were one of the first people I met in this book world as a hopeful author and you helped me become a real one. Thank you for your hand holding, sound boarding, and all your wonderful talents in designing my cover, my teasers, formatting and editing, and everything in between. This book marked a lot of firsts for us. More to come! #DreamTeam.

Prologue

MIA COLLINS

"Leave me alone!" I hear someone scream, their voice so loud it frightens me awake, my heart beating out of my chest. I rush out of the room, slowly creeping down the stairs. As I near the final step, I hear sobbing followed by smashing glass. Initially, I think it's an intruder, but the closer I get, the more familiar the voices become. I make my way in the direction of the kitchen, and when I get there, I see my mother standing next to the kitchen counter in the pajamas she had put on after dinner. She isn't smiling as she had been a few hours ago, though. Tears streak her cheeks. She looks tired—both physically and emotionally.

In front of her, barely standing, is my father. He is dressed in a button-down that has come untucked from his dark blue jeans. On the floor between them are broken pieces of glass. Even from where I'm standing I can recognize the "Jack Daniels" label on what is left of the bottle. To my knowledge, my parents had never fought before, and watching them now feels as if I'm watching strangers—not my parents. I sense something is breaking, and it isn't just the bottle on the floor…

COLTON HUNTER

"Damn it."

I can*not* believe I left my laptop at home. At least that's where I assume it is. The last place I'd seen the damn thing was in my room. Yesterday, I had packed everything and moved in early to the fraternity house on account of football practice starting before classes did.

I need my computer to finish an assignment for the independent studies course I enrolled in this summer. It's for advanced students and I decided to take it because I thought it would look good on my transcript, and help with graduate school applications if football doesn't work out.

I think about who could bring it to me so that I don't have to drive back home. My football and volleyball playing twin brother and sister, Nick and Kaitlyn, have already moved into their own fraternity and sorority houses, so they're out. I dial my dad's number, but hang up almost immediately when I remember he's at the office, as usual. I decide to call Mom instead. The phone rings until I get her voicemail. Knowing she's probably at the country club planning some form of charitable event—her new hobby—I hang up the phone and decide to pick up the computer myself, even if I'm cutting it a little close to being late for practice.

Fifteen minutes later, I'm home. I let myself into the house and jog up to my room, where I immediately spot my laptop. I grab it and the charger, then look around to make sure I'm not forgetting anything else. After running down a mental checklist, I close my door and head down the hall towards the stairs. As I approach the staircase, I hear a sound coming from my parents' bedroom. I continue walking, but stop when I hear a man's voice; the tone and pitch not like my father's. My stomach begins to ache. Something bad is about to happen. I can feel it in my gut. Letting out a breath, I push one foot in front of the other, let myself into my parents' room, and cannot erase what I see from my mind …

Chapter One

One Year Later…

MIA

"Mia, hurry up! We're going to be late," my roommate, Kiya, yells at me through the bathroom door. Although I can safely say that after spending the whole summer living with her, she is more than just my roommate—she's my closest friend. After transferring to Bragan University from California in June, I'd moved into the dorms to take some summer classes.

That was when I met Kiya for the first time. She'd walked into the room, announced that she was my roommate and that we were "going to be the best of friends". I thought she was kidding, but after a few days of sharing the space with her, I realized she was not. She was right though; she did become my best friend.

"Mia! Hello?"

Crap.

"I'm getting ready!" I yell back. "Ugh, why did I agree to go to this bar?" I add.

"Because you survived your first semester at Bragan!" Kiya shouts back. "And you've been hauling ass this entire summer, so we are celebrating! We are partying, and drinking, and maybe bringing some guys back to the dorm!" she says in a very cheery voice. She sounds like she's already started drinking, but I'm not going to say anything. She deserves the break after working so hard to catch up on classes. I haven't been the only one hitting the books this summer.

I rush to get ready, running to my closet to grab my favorite pair of jean shorts. They aren't anything fancy, but they make me feel comfortable. It's still warm outside, so I put on black strappy sandals, and throw on a black tank top. I check myself out in the mirror and think I look okay, but when Kiya comes out of the bathroom, I can see from her expression that I don't. Her eyes travel from the messy bun at the top of my head to my feet. I know she disapproves of what I am wearing, but I don't care. I agreed to go to this thing, but I never agreed to dress up for it.

Kiya on the other hand looks amazing. She is wearing tight leather jeans and an off-the-shoulder black t-shirt. I know I'm going to end up coming back to the dorm alone. I'm a little jealous that Kiya, unlike myself, inherited her father's darker skin, while I only inherited an almost permanent tan.

"Really? That's what you are going to wear?" she finally says to me.

"Yup. I told you I was going to the stupid bar, but you never said anything about a dress code."

She sighs in defeat. "Ugh, fine, Mia. Let's go. The Uber is outside already."

I manage to grab my purse before Kiya pulls me out of the room. This night is one of the last nights we will be spending in this dorm. We looked at a loft over the summer and are finally moving in on September first.

By the time the Uber finally stops in front of the bar, Eclipse, I begin feeling very uncomfortable. I can see cars parked all around the building. This place is clearly packed, and the thought of walking in there to a large crowd of people overwhelms me. Classes and the dorm are where I've spent my summers. Bars, parties, and large groups terrify me. Still, I swallow my fear, pushing it down as far as it can go.

One day of doing something different won't kill me.

Before I'm able to second guess my decision, I am once again manhandled by Kiya. She is a little too eager to get inside, and almost runs into the bouncer in the process. He asks for our IDs, and since I am only twenty, I give him the fake ID Kiya made me get a few weeks ago. She hands him hers, but she's got nothing to worry about since she's twenty-one. He inspects the IDs, then looks directly at us. My stomach sinks, and the fear that we'll get caught creeps in. He returns the IDs and gestures for us to go inside.

As soon as we get inside, Kiya disappears from my side. I assumed she would, but I expected us to at least have drinks in our hands before she did. I guess I was wrong.

I glance around the room, taking in my surroundings. I like to be aware, especially when I'm somewhere unfamiliar.

In the middle of the room, there is a dance floor that is too small for the number of people currently dancing on it. There is no DJ, but there are large speakers in different places on the ceiling. The music is so loud that I can barely hear my own thoughts. Kiya lied by telling me this was a bar since it's definitely a nightclub. Of course, my roommate would have known I'd reject an invitation to a nightclub instantly. I roll my eyes, disappointed at myself for falling for it.

I move further into Eclipse and make my way to the bar. I stand there for about twenty minutes before I finally catch the attention of one of the bartenders. I ask him for a Malibu rum and Coke. I've never been much of a drinker, but that's the drink

I remember my mom getting when we went out to eat. I'm out, so might as well try it. Plus, I know Kiya will be mad at me if my breath doesn't at least smell like alcohol. If I'm going to pay for a drink, it might as well be one my mother enjoyed.

After downing a second drink, which ended up not being awful, I spot Kiya. She is in the middle of the dance floor, dancing up on some guy who seems to be thoroughly enjoying it. His hands are low on her hips as she swings them to the beat. I envy her sometimes. She is careless, fearless, and puts herself out there. She makes sure she is always herself regardless of what others may think. But I know I can't be like her, because I'm not fearless, or careless. I'd like to think I don't care about what others think, but deep down, I know I do.

In an attempt to drown my thoughts, I look down at my phone, which is funny because aside from Kiya, there is no one else I talk to. No one else even has my number. I carry one for the sole purpose of calling 911 in case of an emergency. I look at the time and notice I've been sitting here for two hours, though it doesn't feel like it. Lucky for me, no one approaches me or even attempts to start a conversation. It's as if I'm invisible, which is fine. I prefer it this way.

I put my phone away and begin to look around the room again, searching for Kiya. She has moved to a corner and is taking shots with three guys. One has his hands wrapped around her waist, while the other two are laughing. I can't tell what's being said, but it must be one hell of a story. I keep looking around, not for anything in particular—just to take it all in. My eyes stop on a girl pretty enough to be a model. She appears to be around 5'7 or 5'8 with corn silk blonde hair that falls smoothly below her shoulders. Her black mini skirt makes her long muscular legs look all the more lengthy and attractive. She's also wearing a red crop top and her look is complete with a smoky-eye and red lipstick.

When she tries to make her way to the dance floor, she starts to wobble on her feet. She's probably drunk like everyone else in here. Everyone but me. Two guys approach, both towering over her. They block her path and begin to touch her. One grabs her from behind and the other gets close to her face. They are too close to her, and she is visibly uncomfortable. She tries to push the one in front of her away, trying to get him to stop blocking the path, but her efforts are unsuccessful. She isn't sober enough or strong enough to succeed. No one rushes to her aid, so she is either alone, or her friends aren't paying attention to her. There are too many people at Eclipse, yet everyone is too busy minding their own business. They either haven't noticed or don't care enough to do something, but for some reason I do.

But how can I help her? I'm a short one-hundred-and-twenty-pound girl. I cannot pick a fight with these guys. They're pissing me off, though, staring at this girl like she's their prey, their dinner. Still, I can't let these guys take advantage of her. My feet start moving. With each step I take, I whisper to myself, "You got this, Mia."

"Hey!" I yell at the two douchebags who don't even realize I'm standing here. The girl looks at me though, and I can see the plea in her eyes. She's afraid and with good reason.

"Hello? Can you hear me?" I raise my voice and wave my arms, while making sure I exude a confidence I certainly don't feel.

"You want in on some of the action?" asks one of the jerks. He turns to face me, lowering his face to meet my eyes. His pupils are dilated and his eyes are red. Yup, he's got to be on something.

I decide to change my approach. As I get ready to execute my new plan I am pushed and shoved by others grinding on the dance floor. After pushing and shoving others out of my way, I finally reach them and, instead of having an all-out battle with these guys in the middle of the dance floor, I grab the girl's hand and drag her outside.

"Stop!" the girl shouts at me as she tries to wrench her arm out of my hold. We stop in the parking lot beside the bar, and I release my grip on her arm.

"Who the hell do you think you are?" she asks as she glares at me. I am not sensing an ounce of gratitude from her even though I'm pretty sure I just prevented her from getting assaulted.

"Can you speak?" she demands angrily.

I don't know what her problem is with me, but her tone is starting to annoy me.

"I can speak, and I don't think I'm the one you should be yelling at right now considering I just helped you," I say to her, looking her straight in the eyes. For a brief second, I wonder if I should have even bothered to help her at all. I shake that thought out of my mind immediately. No one deserves to get assaulted.

"Help me?" she splutters. "What… Why… I didn't need your help!" She yelps as she loses her balance, only catching herself just before hitting the ground. I'm not sure if she's too drunk or too naïve to realize what could've happened to her tonight.

I don't say anything in response. I know I have to get her home. She's vulnerable, and someone else could take advantage of her.

"Mia!" I hear Kiya say from behind me. "What happened?" she asks, panting. "I was dancing and when I looked around for you to introduce you to a few guys, you were hauling ass out of the bar with some—"

Before Kiya could finish her sentence, she stops and stares at the girl, then looks to me. Her eyes widen, and I realize she knows this girl.

"Mia, why did you drag Kaitlyn Hunter out of the bar?" This time she speaks to me with a different tone; she's curious.

"Some douchebags were trying to take advantage of her. She's hammered so I brought her outside," I grudgingly explain.

"I'm not drunk," Kaitlyn says. Kiya and I turn to see Kaitlyn clutch her stomach. She bends over and begins to throw up. Great. This night just went from celebratory to disturbing.

We watch Kaitlyn intently, waiting for her to stop throwing up. She lifts her head after she finishes, and I can see the relief in her eyes. I guess getting some of the alcohol out of her system was helping.

"Where are her friends?" Kiya asks, echoing the question I asked myself earlier.

I shrug and answer, "I think she came alone. I didn't see anyone with her, or around her. And if she did come with someone, they're long gone by now."

Kiya looks puzzled for a moment before shaking her head. "We have to get someone to pick her up," she says and I nod in agreement. Kiya turns to Kaitlyn and asks for her phone. After Kaitlyn hands it over, Kiya says she's going to call Kaitlyn's brother. Kaitlyn goes pale at the thought, but Kiya is already searching through the contacts. Before I can ask Kiya how she knows the girl's brother, Kiya waves the phone at me and puts it to her ear.

I can't hear whatever Kiya is saying while she's on the phone because now I am too busy holding Kaitlyn's blonde locks back while she continues to empty the contents of her stomach. I am so grossed out that I almost join her. I promise myself to never be the girl that gets this drunk.

"He's on his way," Kiya says as she joins us on the sidewalk. Kaitlyn has stopped throwing up, but she needs a shower and sleep. I watch as she sits hunched over on the ground, her head resting on her knees. She has no fight left in her. She is ready to go home. And honestly, so am I.

COLTON

"Are you kidding me?" I ask out loud as I am woken by my ringing phone. I pry my eyes open and look at the alarm clock on my nightstand. It's almost 2 a.m. I rub my eyes, lift myself up from the bed and grab my phone. I look at the caller I.D., finding Chase is calling. I know something is wrong because if anyone knows not to wake me up, it's my best friend.

"What do you want, Boulder?" I demand. The guys had gone out tonight, but I was exhausted from extra football practices and finishing an assignment, so I decided to stay home.

"Colton, you need to get your ass here right now!" Chase responds seriously.

I jump out of bed and start searching for some clothes. "Where are you? What's going on?" I put on my sweats, and search around for a sweatshirt.

"It's Nick," Chase says. Those words are like a bucket of cold water. I'm alert now. I feel my jaw harden, and I start to wonder what's happened to my brother. He's always getting into trouble, and I have to get him out of it. I'm his big brother. I'm the one that looks out for him, but damn, sometimes it gets tiring.

"Are you waiting for an invitation to continue?" I snap. "What the hell happened to Nick?"

"We were at Thompson's place. Nick had a few too many drinks and started flirting with one of the girls at the party. Her boyfriend showed up and a fight broke out. I tried to break up the fight," he says in one breath.

"Where are you now?" I demand. I know he's got more to tell me, and the fact that he isn't right now is pissing me off.

"The police showed up and arrested Nick and the other guy. I'm on my way to the police station." My brother got himself arrested. Again.

If they call my parents, I'll never hear the end of it.

As if sensing my thoughts Chase adds, "I told him not to call your parents. I told him I was going to call you and we'd get him out."

I'm out the door by the time he finishes his sentence. I have my keys in hand, all semblance of sleep gone and replaced by rage. I tell Chase I'll meet him at the station. I get in my car and speed off.

Ten minutes later, I park my car at the empty station, and run inside. I find Chase sitting in a chair, his elbows resting on his knees, and his hands covering his eyes. There's dried blood on his knuckles. He'd thrown some punches, but clearly hadn't been arrested.

He lifts his head and looks directly at me.

"Hey, Colton."

I walk towards him as he slowly stands from his chair and meets me halfway.

"You okay?" I direct my eyes to his knuckles. He follows my gaze and nods.

"Yeah, you should see the other guy," he says with a smirk.

"Why wasn't anyone else arrested?" I ask.

He looks down at the floor avoiding my eyes. "Because when the police came, the rest of us stopped fighting, but Nick and the boyfriend kept going at it." I know Chase wishes he'd stopped the fight, but I also know how stubborn my brother is.

"Okay, let's get the idiot out of here," I respond, walking towards the front desk like I have too many times before.

I talk to the clerk—a middle-aged woman whose eyes never leave my body—and after what feels like half an hour, my brother is let out. They don't book him, or file any paperwork. They just wanted to hold him, to get him to calm down. This isn't the first time my brother has ended up here, but his charm, reputation, and skill on the field make even the police feel bad about getting him in trouble.

Isn't he lucky?

I thank the clerk and walk out of the police station with my brother in front of me. He has a busted lip, but all in all, it seems he won the fight. Part of me is angry that he got into a stupid brawl, and I had to run and bail him out. The other part is proud that I taught him how to defend himself.

We get in the car and I begin driving back home. Nick and Chase are talking, but I am not paying any attention to them. I am exhausted and ready for bed.

"I could have finished that guy if the cops hadn't come in and broken us up," Nick says smugly. "And I would've been screwing his girlfriend right now, too."

His words snap me out of my stupor and I narrow my eyes at him through the rear-view mirror. He's just sitting there, relaxed—proud of himself. Why can't he see how much trouble he's caused? Why doesn't he give a fuck?

"You need to get your shit together," I say to him, keeping my eyes on the road for a moment before flickering back to his face.

Nick sits up straight, and the shift in the mood is palpable. "I know," he responds, but I know this won't be the last time we'll be having this conversation.

"I don't want to get any more calls about you being in jail because you decided to flirt with some chick at a party." I scold him like a parent would—like a parent should.

"She shouldn't have flirted back. If anything, I was doing the guy a favor. I showed him how easy his girlfriend is." I can see him smiling through the intermittent street lights rolling over the car's interior.

"Yeah, but you're the dumbass that decided to fight her boyfriend, and land your ass in jail," Chase jokes.

"Yeah, yeah." Nick brushes it off, already bored of the conversation. He likes getting into fights. At first, I thought he did it to get our parents, William and Adaline's, attention. They have never been attentive, or caring about what happens to us. But now, I think he just picks fights out of anger. He knows our parents don't care if he's in the hospital or not. They're too worried about themselves, leaving it to me to pick up the slack.

My train of thought is interrupted by my phone ringing. It's 3 a.m. now. I guess the theme of the night is to call Colton and piss him off. I look at the Caller I.D. It's my sister, Kaitlyn.

"Hey, Kay, what's up?" I ask when I answer the call.

"Hey, is this Colton Hunter?" An unfamiliar girl's voice asks on the other end of the line.

"Yeah, who's this?" I practically shout back, my anger flaring. This isn't the first time this has happened. My sister's friends are always calling to flirt with me, or ask me out. It's pathetic.

I'm about to hang up the phone when she says, "My name is Kiya. I'm calling because you need to come and pick up Kaitlyn."

"Pick her up from where, and why?" I ask, fearing what her answer is. I'm still annoyed from having to deal with my brother, and now this? This is a night from hell.

"We're at Eclipse. She's hammered and throwing up. None of her friends are here," the girl says.

"Fuck," I mutter under my breath.

Kaitlyn likes going to Eclipse. I never go there. It's a tacky bar with sketchy people. I'm so tired that I just want to find my bed, but I know I'm not going to anytime soon. My sister needs me to pick her up. I take the next left turn, and start heading towards Eclipse.

Everybody needs rescuing tonight.

I guess I'm on call.

Chapter Two

MIA

After what feels like a thirty-minute wait, I spot a black Camaro approaching the club. I've always loved Camaros. They are sexy and mysterious. I can admire a beauty when I see it, and this car is definitely one that captures your attention, and makes you want to look. As I stare at the Camaro, it comes to an abrupt stop in front of us.

The windows of the car are tinted, probably too dark to be legal, and though I try, I can't make out anyone inside it. Suddenly, the door opens and a man steps out.

I can't help but watch. He's a giant, and you can tell he takes his workout seriously. His arms are so built that I can make out the muscles through his sweatshirt. I bet all the girls run after him. Well, muscles are not enough to impress me. He closes the distance, walking directly towards me. Who is this guy?

I command myself to stop watching him. He isn't my type, not even close. Not that I know what my type is with my limited experience and all, but I know it isn't him. And I am most definitely *not his type.*

"Are you serious?" The guy shouts while standing in front of Kaitlyn. She lowers her head, avoiding his questioning eyes.

This is Kaitlyn's brother?

"I'm fine, Colton," she responds bringing her eyes back up to his.

"Really, you're fine? I get a phone call from a stranger saying that I need to pick you up because you're too drunk to take care of yourself, and you're standing here saying you're fine!"" He seems frustrated, and I can empathize. He's probably mad he had to leave whatever party he was at because of Kiya's call.

Kaitlyn opens her mouth to respond, but before she can utter a word, Colton grabs her by the arm and pulls her in the direction of his car. He bumps into me as he walks past, knocking me to the side. I throw my hands out in front of me to stop myself from falling to the ground.

"Excuse you!" I yell at him as he continues to walk in the direction of his car like he didn't even notice what he just did. I straighten myself up, and rub my shoulder trying to numb the aching pain.

"Get over it," he says in a hard voice.

Asshole.

What kind of idiot doesn't even thank the strangers for helping his sister out.

Ungrateful imbecile.

I turn to Kiya, looking for support, and I realize she too had been watching his every move. Her gaze lifts to me, and she sends me a silent message to calm down. I nod. I'm normally not one to react, but I want to. I am livid. I am in pain. I keep telling myself that it's because he plowed into me and didn't seem to care, but I know it's because for once I want someone to notice me. Not just anyone, though. I want him to notice me.

I hear a door slam, and then another, followed by the Camaro speeding away. I stand there, staring in its direction until it's out of sight, thinking of what else I could have said.

"He is so hot!" Kiya exclaims, my attention snapping back to the present.

"I didn't notice," I lie.

"Yeah right!" Kiya sees right through my lie, like she always does, but I am not about to admit to anything more. So, I evade the topic.

"He's an asshole," I state matter-of-factly.

"Yeah, well that asshole can take me home any day he wants."

I roll my eyes at her comment, telling myself that I'd happily decline if given the opportunity.

"How do you know him?" I say, trying not to sound too interested. I don't want to think about him, but I want to know more, and see if my roommate has had any encounters with him. I could just hear my mom now: *No como ni dejo comer.* It was something she always said to me when I didn't want something, but also didn't want anyone else to have it either. That is how I feel about him. Colton. The mannerless imbecile.

Kiya and I decide to call it a night. We still hadn't finished packing.

"Have you loaded the last box?" I ask Kiya. We've spent the afternoon packing the rental van, and making sure everything was out of the dorm. We're finally moving to our own place—my place really—but I am happy to share it with Kiya. As much as I tell myself I like being alone, I really don't.

"Yeah, I just got the last box. There is nothing left. At all."

"I am not looking forward to unpacking." I laugh. "But I am looking forward to finally keeping some wine in the house."

"Oh yeah, we're getting wine wasted tonight," she responds, shifting the car into drive and pulling out into traffic.

It sounds like a wonderful night—unpacking with my roommate, and having some wine and laughs while we're at it.

We arrive at the loft a few minutes later. I wanted to be close enough to walk to class every day, since walking helps me clear my head. We spend two hours pulling out boxes from the rental. That little room we shared had a lot more stuff than we thought. When we finally finish unloading the van, my roommate drops into the black leather couch, and I take a seat on the piano bench. I bought a few things with some of the money my mother had left me to make this loft feel more like a home.

"Wow," Kiya says, looking around. "I can't believe this is where we live," she exclaims.

"I know, right?" I am equally in awe.

"Mia, thanks so much for letting me live with you. You didn't have to, but I'm so glad you did."

"I can't imagine living with anyone else," I say reassuringly. It's true though; I enjoy living with her. "Anyway, let's keep it moving! We have to put it all away now," I say and Kiya groans.

Two hours later, all our boxes are unpacked, and everything is in its proper place. Kiya decides to make dinner and puts me in charge of setting the table and getting drinks. I pour two glasses of white wine for us, and take a seat on the stool in the kitchen to watch her cook. She looks just like my mom and my mind can't help but drift to a memory of her.

I was sitting at the dining room table, and my mother was in the kitchen. She was making my favorite meal for lunch, arroz blanco con camarones. I was home for the long Christmas break after spending freshmen year in school. I hadn't wanted to live on campus, but my mother insisted, telling me that although she would miss me, I needed to have the full college experience.

"Mia, la comida estara lista en cinco minutos." My mother turned around and looked at me as she said this. She knew I was waiting, and impatiently at that. I was tired of burgers, fries, and pizza, and ready for some soul

food—some of the delicious native foods my mother made.

No. Don't think about the past. Don't let it creep up on you. It starts with good memories, but the bad ones follow, the voice at the back of my mind insists.

Don't let it take over, Mia. You know better.

And with that, I come back to the present. Kiya has finished making dinner, and we take our seats at the dining table. The first meal, it's like a christening. It feels amazing, liberating and right. The place looks wonderful, and I get to enjoy it with my best friend. This feeling of peace is what confirms that I made a good decision in moving to Forest Pines. The place I used to call home no longer held the people that made it my haven. Now, there was only emptiness.

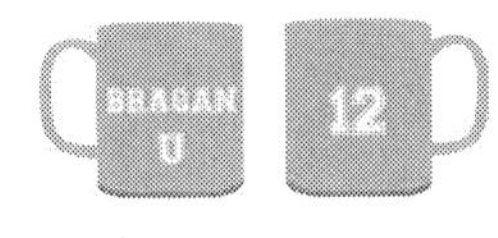

Chapter Three

MIA

Monday mornings, oh how I dislike thee!

I lift my hand and slam it down on the alarm clock. It doesn't matter how good of a student I am; any morning that I have to wake up at six-thirty is a morning I will wake up angry. I promised myself that I wouldn't take any morning classes. Apparently, I couldn't keep this promise since every session of my Junior Seminar class is at 8:00 a.m.

Mornings here I come, I think drily.

I get up from bed and hiss. My whole body is sore from lifting boxes all day yesterday. I massage one shoulder gently then set about choosing what I'm going to wear—not that I particularly care. I pick out a long black shirt, light blue jeans, and black boots. Despite my general indifference to fashion, there is one thing I am obsessed with: shoes. I love boots, and fall is the perfect time to bring them all out. Fall in New England is breathtaking.

I head to the bathroom, brush my teeth, hop in the shower, then get dressed. The house is eerily quiet, and I try not to add any extra noise. I know Kiya will probably sleep until ten since she never takes early classes. She's a senior and the Junior Seminar class wasn't a requirement this year. She doesn't have to experience the nightmare that is waking up at the ass-crack of dawn, also known as 6:30 a.m.

I wish I was her right now.

I walk over to the kitchen, and realize that we barely have anything to eat since we didn't go grocery shopping. The food we made yesterday was what was leftover in the dorm. If I leave now, I can still make it to the coffee shop at school. Coffee is a must; it is the college student's drug of choice. And if I am going to make it through this class, I need a hit. I grab my book bag and walk out.

The school coffee shop is always busy, but I manage to get something hot and caffeinated and a chocolate chip muffin with more than enough time to spare. Since I've been taking classes over the summer, I easily find the building and classroom where my seminar is taking place. I make it to class with fifteen minutes until class starts, which is my goal since I like marking my space.

I feel a little nervous to finally feel the fullness of campus. Not a lot of people take summer classes, so I haven't been exposed to Bragan U. in its thirty thousand strong capacity. Even as I was walking to class, I saw students everywhere. I can't help but feel a little out of place. Bragan is a large school, yet everyone seems to know everyone…except me.

"Okay class," says a middle-aged man from the front of the room.

My head jerks up at the sound of his voice, and the din of the classroom fills my ears. I hadn't even realized I wasn't alone anymore.

"My name is James Clift and I will be your professor for this course. As you all know, this is Junior Seminar, and though I'd like to think you all enrolled in this class because you want to learn, I know better to know that it is a required course that needs to be taken before senior year."

The class laughs as the professor begins to pass out the syllabus.

He gives a stack to each person in the front row and asks us to pass it back. When I look behind me, I realize that the class isn't too large—*maybe* thirty students at most. I focus my attention back to the professor, who is now standing to the left of the board.

"Unlike most of your classes, in this class you will be graded based on group work."

As those words leave his mouth, everyone in the class begins to utter complaints. I hate group work. I hate the fact that my grades depend on other students, and for some reason, with my luck, I always get stuck with the dumb ones and end up doing all the work.

"I will be assigning the groups on Wednesday, and we will start the first part of our assignment then. The purpose of this class is to select an international problem and ultimately make a proposal as to how to resolve it. This is supposed to help your humanitarian side," the professor continues.

After that revelation, the rest of the class is easy. The professor explains the syllabus, and by explain, I mean he reads each line out loud. It's completely unnecessary since none of us are paying attention. I won't complain though. It stops the professor from teaching the first day of class. Every once in a while, I can hear a student chuckle or gasp about something the professor says.

I guess some people are paying attention.

Professor Clift is desperately trying to be funny, which is refreshing. At least he isn't trying to bore us to death like others do.

"Oh, I almost forgot. Since this is a required class, I do have to take attendance," the professor says just as he is about to dismiss us. Pulling out a piece of paper, he begins calling out names and I tune out, too distracted by the idea of having to do group work in order to pass the course.

"Mia Collins," the professor says. "Ms. Collins are you here?"

With a jolt, I realize I haven't answered him. "Here!" I say to the professor. He sighs like he thinks I'm an idiot for making him call my name twice.

From the corner of my eye, I can see few heads have turned my way. I'm flustered, and slowly slouch down into my seat to escape their eyes. The professor continues going through the attendance sheets, and my thoughts wander off until...

"Colton Hunter," the professor says.

What? I look up, panicked.

"Colton Hunter," Clift repeats, visibly annoyed. I sink deeper into my chair. The professor scans the room briefly before he nods. One of the girls beside me turns around and looks at the brunette sitting next to her, whispering how hot Colton is.

Oh, God. It's definitely him.

Out of all places and all classes, fate has it that I am stuck in class with him. The memory of Saturday night comes flooding back, but I push it away. My shoulder aches a little serving as a reminder that I should not waste another second thinking about that bad-mannered asshole.

Class ends after the professor finishes taking attendance. All the students get up and collect their belongings. Chatter fills the room; everyone is catching up and talking about their summer. I gather my things and stuff them into my book bag. I stand up and as I start walking to the exit, I run into someone, knocking something out of their hands.

"Oh, I'm so sorry," I say to the person I bumped into, not quite looking at them, the pain in my shoulder increasing. I bend down to pick up a notebook from the floor. When I look up, I realize I've bumped into none other than Colton Hunter, and it's his notebook I'm holding. Before he has a chance to speak, I push the notebook into his chest and walk away. I don't really want to engage in conversation with him. If I'd realized it was him I'd bumped into, I would have simply walked away.

I have two more classes left before this day ends. Mondays are going to be hectic since I am taking three courses back-to-back, but hey, I will literally do anything to get Friday's off and enjoy a long weekend of relaxation. Maybe if I motivate myself, I may even get to play the piano.

The rest of my classes go by smoothly. We get our syllabus, talk about the course and requirements, and then get dismissed for the day. The course load seems like it will be manageable, and I know I'm going to do well.

Chapter Four

COLTON

I'm done with classes for the day, and I haven't been able to stop thinking about the girl from earlier—the girl in the seminar class. She'd run into me, apologized sincerely, but then when she saw it was me, her eyes turned from sympathy to something else—pure disdain. I've never seen her before, yet the look she gave me makes me think she knows who I am.

"Yo, Colt, you here?" I hear Zack say. Zack Hayes is one of my fraternity brothers, and an offensive lineman. We share a house with the other team members, among them my brother. Zack is what we like to call the player of the group. Different girl every day, and sometimes every night. Despite that, he's still one of the better guys in the house.

Honestly, there are a few others that are assholes who I'd never voluntarily choose to be friends let alone live with, but I have no choice since it comes with football. I guess one of the good things about sharing a house is that I get to keep an eye on Nick. The way I see it, my brother plus unsupervised athletes' house equals trouble. It also comes with additional perks: parties, drinks, and all the girls we'd ever need.

Not that I sleep around. Not anymore, anyway.

I am no longer a fan of the girls who throw themselves at me. Most of them just want to say we hooked up so they can tell other girls they had sex with a football player—with the quarterback of the football team. I'm not up for that shit anymore. It's my junior year—the most important year of my college career, and contrary to popular belief, I actually want to graduate with honors. Still, I can't say I've never taken advantage of the benefits that came with my reputation, because I have. But that was before.

"Yes, I am." We're sitting in the dining hall, trays filled with food in front of us. A fraternity comprised of all football players means that when we aren't partying, studying, training, or working out, we are eating like starved pigs.

"Dude, did you hear anything I just said?" he asks, and honestly I haven't.

"Do I ever listen to anything you say?" I retort, not admitting to him that I'm thinking about a girl. It might give him the wrong idea.

"Haha, very funny. But seriously, are we still throwing the party on Saturday? We have to welcome in the fresh meat!"

Every semester, the Football House throws a huge start of the semester party where we invite everyone on campus. The Greek system is pretty big at Bragan, and we basically run it because football is at the top of the food chain. The Football House is the most popular fraternity on campus, and the most exclusive one too considering you have to be a football player to get in.

I didn't want to be a part of it, but if I was going to be forced, then I needed to be at the top, which is why I became the president. I needed to be the authority. I needed to be in control.

"We do it every year, don't we?" I shoot back.

"This time we have to go big. It's your first year as president and captain," Zack says, ignoring my sarcastic response.

Nick, Chase, Blake Miller, and Jesse Falcon join our table,

setting down their trays. Blake is the fighter of the group. While I can fight, I don't pick fights. Blake, on the other hand, is very similar to Nick—he loves to start them. I guess that's why they've been inseparable since they started college two years ago. Jesse is the moral compass of the group. He is a pre-med student, who is always the designated driver. He can still party like the best and worst of us, but he has a sharp focus with a clear goal in mind. He's also our main kicker. With all six of us sitting at the table, we are drawing an audience. I hate the unnecessary attention. It feels like we're animals in a zoo, paintings in a museum, clowns at a circus.

The guys talk animatedly about the details of the party. I join the conversation as they begin to joke and laugh about shit from the weekend. The fight is brought up, and me having to bail out my siblings. I can laugh about it now, but I was fuming when it happened.

Speaking of my sister, I see Kaitlyn and her friends making their way to our table. They tend to sit with us because Kaitlyn is family, and also because the guys find the rest of the girls that come with her hot. Kaitlyn is part of a sorority on campus, DM. I don't know what it stands for, and honestly I don't care. With a less than maternal mother when we were growing up, I can see why K's happy to have sisters, even if they aren't blood.

"Hey, guys," Kaitlyn greets us.

"Hey, K," I respond and the rest of the guys voice their own greetings as she takes a seat next to Jesse and joins the conversation. Her friend, Jade, sits next to her, while Abbigail Brown, the head of DM, slides in between Zack and me.

Scooting closer to me, she whispers, "Hey, sexy," in my ear.

Like I said, I don't sleep around, but Abby and I had an understanding. I ended it last weekend, though, when she started acting like she was my girlfriend. I told her from the beginning that I didn't want a relationship. It was only sex, but she got clingy and the arrangement had to end. I don't want to break any girl's heart—I'm not an asshole—but I don't want to be with anyone either, not when I know how deceiving women can be.

"Hello, Abby," I say to her as politely as I can. She slides her hand below the table and rests it on my thigh…

Too close.

I grab her wrist, stopping her before she reaches her goal. She pouts. If she thinks I'll change my mind, she's got another thing coming. I know that sitting next to her will inevitably lead to drama. I don't know if she's the type to make a scene, but it wouldn't be the first time a girl does, and I don't need that right now. I stand up, pick my book bag up from the floor and my tray from the table.

I'm done here.

Chapter Five

MIA

The rest of Tuesday flies by, and Wednesday arrives way too quickly for my liking. It's time for Junior Seminar—time to avoid Colton. With coffee in hand, I walk into the room. I need as much caffeine as I can get to help me through this. With at least fifteen minutes before class begins, I grab my phone and search through the apps until I find a game to play.

The room fills up quickly, the volume of chatter increasing steadily. When the room goes quiet, I assume the professor is here and put my phone away. When I lift my eyes, though, I realize everyone has shut up because Colton has come into the room.

I swear it's like in one of those cheesy movies, where time stops and there is a spotlight on the hot male lead. Still, I can't tear my eyes away. I look from his feet to his dark hair. He has this *just rolled out of bed look,* but it works for him. If I'd just rolled out of bed, it would not be pretty. In sweatpants and a tight-fitting Under Armor shirt that emphasizes the size and shape of his biceps, he looks better than the first time I saw him.

Before I'm able to stop myself, I gaze up and down his body once more and then zero in on his eyes. They are a deep piercing gray, and just like quicksand, I feel myself getting sucked in. He looks over at me, then, catching me watching. My cheeks flush with color and he smiles a perfect smile, then winks. He slowly walks past me, finding a seat at the back of the room.

I'm still frozen from embarrassment, and if I weren't sitting down right now, I would look absurd. I can't believe he caught me blatantly checking him out. I don't even like him. He's handsome, but I would never willingly choose to be romantically involved with him. Not that I imagine he does romantic, but that's beside the point. My cheeks are still red, and I silently pray that no one else noticed.

I force myself to look ahead, replaying the whole thing in my head. I know I had the 'deer caught in the headlights' look when he saw me. And his reaction showed me that he knew exactly what I was doing. I mean, his response was to smile and wink mockingly at me.

Arrogant jerk.

After what feels like forever, the professor finally enters the classroom.

"Okay class. Settle down," Clift says as he gestures with his hands for the students to sit down. "I need you all to get into groups of no more than three students. Once you're in those groups, we will do an activity which will allow me to take attendance and hopefully learn your names."

I am instantly frightened. Had I misheard him? I sit there for a moment, waiting for him to assign groups.

"You have four minutes," Professor Clift adds. "I suggest you start."

While everyone else gets up from their seats and move to their friends, I sit there. I figure someone will move towards me eventually. But as the minutes pass, I begin to feel like the kid in the movies—the one that always gets picked last in gym class, or the one that the teacher has to force someone to add to their teams. Yup, that will be me. The lame one. The last pick. The one no one wants. I gotta say, this is not a foreign feeling.

"Did everyone find a group?" the professor asks after the allotted time. He looks around the room, and sees the groups that have been formed. I don't want to raise my hand and show him that I'm not in a group, but it's kind of obvious. I'm sitting in the front of the class, and no one else is around me.

"Miss, what was your name again?" Professor Clift says. I hope for half a second he isn't talking to me, but I can see him staring.

"Mia," I say. "Mia Collins."

"Yes, Mia," he says, emphasizing my name.

The professor looks around the room again, then turns his attention back to me and says, "I think Mr. Hayes's group can fit one more. Mr. Hayes and Mr. Hunter, thank you for volunteering."

No. No. No! This can't be happening.

The professor is staring at me. "Miss Collins, please join Mr. Hunter and Mr. Hayes."

I'm trying to but my feet aren't cooperating. They're stuck in place. I regret not standing up earlier and adding myself to a team. Even if it would have been uncomfortable, it would have been better than this. This is what I get for being a coward.

The professor lifts his glasses and his eyebrows follow, and I take that as a signal to get up. I grab my notebook, throw my book bag over my left shoulder, and turn to face the back of the room. Legs trembling, I make my way up the stairs and that's when I realize that all eyes are on me.

The guys in the room are giving me amused looks, while the girls eye me with anger and jealousy.

There goes the invisibility cloak, I think to myself. I'm the center of attention, and I don't like it one bit. I make my way to the back of the room as quickly as I possibly can, hoping that the sooner I get there, the quicker the scrutinizing eyes will be off me. I'm forced to look up in order to figure out exactly where I'll be sitting, when all of a sudden…

Bang!

I trip and go down, but my knee breaks my fall before my face can. Laughter immediately ripples through the room. I have the distinct urge to run, but that would be like a dramatic exit in one of the Telenovelas I used to watch with my mother. That would be even more embarrassing. Even as the laughter in the room gets louder, I pick up my notebook, stand up and lift my chin high.

I catch someone staring at me with a devilish grin. She is a slim girl with blonde hair, green eyes and extremely long legs. She immediately makes me feel self-conscious. She's watching me with satisfaction in her eyes, like she's proud of herself.

"Find your place, Miss. Collins," the professor says impatiently, stopping the staring contest between the girl and me. I nod and continue walking, having to force every step. When I drop down into the empty seat next to Hayes, I don't look at him or Colton. I know my face is still red and hot with embarrassment. I just want this to be over.

COLTON

I find myself watching the girl in the front row, waiting to see what she'll do. What group would she be a part of? A few girls wanted to sit with us, and Zack wanted them to as well, but I gave them a look to keep them away. Last semester, Abby sat with us in every class we shared, but after last weekend, that is no longer the case. It's not that I don't want to be friends with her. I just need her to get over me first.

I keep watching the girl, now sitting alone at the front of the room. She doesn't move from her seat, even when everyone else is finding a group.

"Hey, Colton—" a girl begins to ask in a sugary sweet voice.

"No," I reply, my gaze not leaving my girl.

Zack leans into me. "Hey, give a guy a chance here," he says. I give him a sideways glance. He shrugs. "She's hot."

"It doesn't matter," I reply.

When the girl looks around and sees the groups being formed, she doesn't seek anyone out. Who is she? Where does she come from? And why in the hell did she look at me as if she hates me. I wait until everyone is in a group, and I look at her again. She is still alone.

I'm about to volunteer our group when the professor looks around the room and finds Zack. And almost like an answer to my prayers—or thoughts—Professor Clift makes her join our group. I couldn't have planned it any better. I can't wipe the smug grin off my face either.

After the professor tells her she is going to be a part of my group, she turns her head, her eyes locking onto my face, along with the rest of the class. She looks pissed off. I saw the way she was staring at me when I walked into class today. I thought she'd jump at the chance of working with me.

I must admit, though, I'd enjoyed having her watch me. I don't like it most days, but I liked it when it came from her.

I watch her, studying her every movement. I can see the wheels turning, her hesitation to get up out of her seat. That's when the professor loses his patience and demands that she move. She stands up with her belongings in hand, and I let my gaze rake her body from her open-toe sandals, to her tight faded skinny jeans that have holes in them, and finally to the off-the-wall shirt with a deep V in the front. Forcing myself to look up, I take in her full lips and almond-shaped eyes. She is beautiful–the I don't know I'm pretty kind of beautiful. I smile to myself.

Her eyes downcast, she makes her way up the stairs, only looking up briefly before she lurches forward unexpectedly, landing hard on her knees.

The moment I see her collapse, I jump out of my chair. I want to help her. Still on her hands and knees, she hesitates for a few moments. A big part of me wants to offer my hand, pick up her things, and make sure she's okay. Another part of me remembers how she looked at me, so I don't make a move. I slowly slide back into my chair, the sense of protectiveness still looming over me, but overpowered by my sense of self-preservation.

She gathers her belongings and makes her way to our table. I look away, pretending I hadn't been paying attention. She grabs the empty seat next to Zack, and I'll be damned if I'm not disappointed it isn't next to me instead.

Zack nudges me and gives me a reassuring nod. He knows I don't like having girls in our groups because they never bring much to the table. Girls just sit there, flipping their hair, giggling, and making sure their breasts are pushed together enough to give us a clear view of their cleavage. That shit is annoying, but it's even worse when they pretend to not know anything. Who the hell is attracted to stupid? Certainly not me. I have a future waiting for me after I finish school.

But right now, at this moment, I don't care about my usual resolve. I abandon all reason. Ignore all precedents. I shrug my shoulders, telling Zack I'm indifferent. But I'm not. I'm glad she's in our group. She's a puzzle I am determined to put together.

"Okay, now that everyone has found their groups," Professor C. states, looking directly at our group. From the corner of my eye, I see Mia scoot down in her seat. "The first assignment is for the group members to identify a world problem they would like to resolve. I need to know why the problem is important to each of you because this is the problem you will be working on for the rest of the semester.

You will conduct research, work on a presentation, and submit a paper, which you will try and get published in an undergraduate journal. The problem you choose is the problem you'll be stuck with, so choose wisely. If it's too hard, well, that's what makes it a problem. Try and get to know one another, since you will be inseparable until the end of the semester."

I can't contain the smile that appears on my face; the professor has made these groups permanent and my mission easier.

Chapter Six

MIA

As if my humiliation isn't enough, now we have to work on a semester-long project together, and try and get to know one another like we're in middle school. This is college; we don't need icebreakers, and we don't need group work.

The professor asks us to interview someone in our group. We need to ask each other a few questions like where we come from, how old we are, and our biggest fear. No one needs to know anything about my life, yet my professor expects me to share this information with strangers.

"A sheet with instructions is being distributed. It also contains directions on what the problem you are solving must include. Make sure you choose something everyone in the group is passionate about. To do this, you should get to know one another. This will be your first homework assignment."

The torture has commenced…well, continued. I hope all the group work can be done in class. I hate having to coordinate with other people just as much as I hate being stuck doing all the work.

One of the girls from the group in front of us turns. Her eyes immediately focus on Colton. I notice she has the assignment sheet in her hand. I assume she turned around to pass it to us, but she now finds herself too consumed by Colton.

I clear my throat as loudly as I can to get the girl's attention. The girl looks at me with exasperation, her annoyance visible on her face—like I have rudely interrupted her moment, which is bullshit because in reality she is staring at him and he's having a conversation with Hayes.

"Can I have the instructions?" I ask, directing my gaze at the sheet in her hand. She follows my eyes and immediately pushes out her chest, her mouth curling into a sneaky smile.

Flipping her hair over her shoulder, she says in a manufactured innocent voice, "Hey, Colton." I look to Colton to see what he'll do. He turns, looks in her direction, bobs his head and then returns to his conversation.

At that moment, my heart aches for the girl. He barely acknowledges her. She stares at the side of his head a little longer, then shifts her eyes to me and practically throws the sheet at me. Luckily, I catch it before it drops to the floor, but what does end up dropping is every ounce of sympathy I had for her.

I place the assignment instructions on my desk.

"Okay, students, make sure you share contact information with the rest of your group, read the instructions, and I expect this assignment to be ready by next class, which is Monday." Everyone groans in unison. "Yeah, yeah," the professor continues. "Have a nice weekend." He dismisses the class and is the first one out the door. That's new.

I shoot up from my desk and gather my belongings. Screw this assignment. One missed assignment never hurt anybody. I leave the instruction sheet with questions on the table without even looking at it, and begin to walk down the stairs when I feel a hand grip my arm. Goosebumps break out all over my skin, and I know whose hand it is immediately. I turn to face Colton. I tilt my head back to look him in the eye. Once again, it feels as though time has stopped as his eyes travel my body, searching for something.

I snap back into reality remembering how much of an entitled prick he is, ignoring everyone, being an asshole to people who have attempted to help those that he cares for. I see his mouth curl into a confident smile. Yup, arrogant too. Add that to the long list of negative qualities this guy possesses.

"Can I help you?" I state in the boldest tone I can muster. He stares at me as if he hasn't registered my words. I drop my gaze to his hand, which is still holding both gently and firmly onto my arm. He follows my gaze, and as if he has been shocked by a thousand bolts of lightning, he rapidly releases his fingers. I see concern flash through his eyes. Maybe he thinks he hurt me, but that isn't the case, this time.

"Uh, yeah, actually," he states, scratching the back of his neck with his left hand—a gesture that makes his arm look even bigger, if that's possible. He looks cute and insecure, but I know it must be a trick that he's perfected over the years to make girls fall for him. I'm not buying the act, but I don't mind watching it happen.

"And how's that?" I inquire, partly intrigued, partly annoyed, while trying really hard to look as disinterested as possible.

"Well, I need your phone number." My hand immediately goes to my hip, something my mother used to do. I can't believe he has the guts to ask me for my number when he completely ignored me. I'm about to tell him to screw off when he opens his mouth to speak again.

"Zack and I need it…you know, for the project. We have to figure out a time to get together." He shows me the instruction sheet that he must have picked up from the table. Guess I must look like the kind of girl who doesn't give a crap about schoolwork. I blush. He doesn't want my number for anything more than to work on the assignment—an assignment I had already forgotten about and given up on.

"Ah, yeah, okay." I won't say I'm embarrassed, because I'm far past that by now. He hands me his phone and I put my number into it. When I'm done, I hand it back.

"Okay," he says with a teasing smile. "I'll text you." I nod in agreement. He stands there, not saying anything else. Ready to be done with this shitty day, I turn around and walk away.

Every step I take away from him is like pulling an elastic. I'm afraid I'll be pulled back. I exit the building and try my best to stomp on the butterflies that have taken up permanent residence in my stomach. He probably won't text me. I'll probably be stuck working on this assignment alone, though, I don't see how that's even possible considering he has the assignment sheet, not me. I know this, but even so, I can't eliminate the sliver of hope...hope that he will text me.

COLTON

This week has been shit. Thanks to some of the guys not showing up for practice on Wednesday, we got stuck doing drills at 8 a.m. on Friday. Friday is the day I get to sleep in and actually do my own thing, but here I am. Outside. In the sun, because New England is unpredictable when it comes to the weather so even though its fall, it's as hot as balls.

Today, we are stuck doing laps. It's not like we run cross-country or track, but Coach likes collective punishment. Our defense is slow, and opposing teams run circles around them, making thirty-yard passes, running right through our defense. Don't get me wrong, the guys can tackle, but if a quarterback throws a long enough pass, our guys just can't get there. Offense is left trying to play catch up every time. And although I can make passes, you need both a good offense and defense to win games. You need a good team. We've been able to keep up, but if we want to win again this year, we have to work on our weaknesses. The other teams have spotted it, and I know they'll use it to their advantage. I sure as hell would.

I've grown up hearing the saying, "You don't want to be the good player on a bad team." I know these guys aren't bad, but they do need to be whipped into shape. So, even though the sun is blinding, and I feel sweat running down my body, I run. I run because I'm the head of this team, and this is the way I lead. That's why we are all here, out on the field, working ourselves to the point of exhaustion.

We have no choice. I have no choice. At least not if I want to go pro. We've had scouts browsing before, but we need to make them stare. We need to give them something to look at. We need to be good enough.

By the time practice is over, I can barely move. I take a shower in the locker room, change, and then check my watch. It's already 4 p.m. We practiced for eight hours, taking some breaks in between. No one complained though. They know it's necessary if we want to be the best.

I make my way to the house and go up to my room, which is as far away from everyone else as I can get. I place my gear bag and book bag next to my desk, and proceed to drop onto the welcoming queen-sized mattress. My muscles ache. I'm worn out and I slowly find myself drifting away.

I wake to the sound of furniture being dragged around. I slowly open my eyes and turn to face the clock. It's 12:30 p.m.

Shit! It's Saturday.

I slept for nineteen hours. Who the hell sleeps for that long? I roll out of bed and make my way to the bathroom. I need a shower, and to brush my teeth. I hear my stomach grumble. Yeah, food. I need food, too.

I finish getting ready and make my way downstairs, where I immediately spot the guys at work. They're never up to do anything, especially work, unless it involves partying. Somehow they get their shit together real quick for a party.

The couches and TV are being moved to the basement so that when things get wild, which they always do, no one can break our furniture. We've been planning tonight's official welcoming party for a week. Unofficially, it's more like a viewing where the guys get to scout the "fresh meat". The new girls. From this party, the guys will try and get a feel for which girls are easy enough to get into bed, and even how many they can get into bed at once.

I'm not interested in that anymore. I took advantage of these parties, and the status that came from both being in the fraternity, and a football player. That's not me anymore.

"Hey, Colt, welcome back to life!" Blake comments.

"Yeah, bro, we were starting to worry," Jesse adds.

"He probably had a girl up there all night. Is she still in there?" Zack gives me a smug grin and lifts his eyebrows.

"Why? You looking for my sloppy seconds?" I tease. As much shit as these guys give me, I love them all. They're family.

"Never. You know I can hold my own," Zack responds.

"I'm pretty sure we've all had your sloppy seconds," Chase adds matter-of-factly. That is probably true. I shrug my shoulders and make my way into the kitchen.

The rest of the day passes by quickly, which is always the case when people are busy. We put anything breakable in the basement. We set up kegs in the kitchen, and a DJ booth in the living room which will double as a dance floor tonight. I run upstairs and take another shower. I'm not really in the partying mood but this is one of the responsibilities that come with being president. I get ready, locking my door behind me. The last thing I need is for someone to sneak up here and get off in my room.

I make my way downstairs, grab a beer and go to the backyard where a fire has been lit. I enjoy being out here in the fall. Fall nights are especially spectacular. The stars are clearly visible, shining brightly in the night sky. This, right here, is one of the reasons I chose to go to school close to home. I would miss New Hampshire too much if I left. This place is home.

MIA

He hasn't texted. He probably isn't going to text. I have been waiting for a message since Wednesday. I thought he'd at least send a message with his contact info, but no. Nothing. Zero, Zip, Nada.

I told myself not to expect it. I mean, sure at first, I thought he might, but who am I kidding? He's probably spent the last three days with a different girl, maybe more than one. Gross. Not that it's any of my business anyway, even if we have this stupid assignment we have to work on together.

"Hey, M, what are you doing?" Kiya says as she lets herself into my room and drops onto my bed.

I signal with my hands at the papers spread all around me. "Well, I was doing homework, but I'm done now." *Almost done anyway,* I think bitterly.

"Okay. Good. Get ready. We're going out," she exclaims, excitement visible in her eyes.

I throw myself on top of the large pillow on my bed. "No, I'm tired." I yawn to prove a point.

"Oh, come on! You need to do something fun. You barely do anything."

"I did something fun like two weekends ago," I whine.

"That's crap and you know it. If you remember correctly, the last time we went out, we couldn't even enjoy ourselves. It involved throw up. You owe me," she states, looking like a little girl throwing a tantrum because she isn't getting what she wants. Her arms are crossed and she's actually pouting. All that's missing is her stomping her foot.

"Don't remind me." The image of Kaitlyn throwing up immediately pops into my brain. I chuckle. That night was something else. That was the night I first ran into Colton…or better said, he ran into me. Shit, why does my mind always go back to him? I feel my will to stay in my room and sleep weakening when I know I'll spend my night thinking about him. I need a distraction, ASAP.

"So?" Kiya questions expectantly.

"Where are we going?" There is no way in hell I'm returning to Eclipse. Not after the last time.

"We're going to a house party. It's a huge party to welcome the freshmen," she states with a triumphant look on her face. I'd used the word 'we', and she knows I'm caving.

"But you aren't a freshman, and neither am I, Kiya." It doesn't make any sense. Why would we show up to a party that is specifically thrown for freshmen?

"Everyone is invited, silly! Plus, you're a transfer student, so you are fresh meat! At least here at B.U."

"Alright, fine. But if I go, you have to promise to stick with me. I don't want to end up on the early morning news."

"The news? Oh, you mean… Yeah, sure, I'll stick with you, but you shouldn't worry. Stuff like that doesn't happen at B.U."

"Yeah, I'm sure that's what most people thought until it happened to them." I truly worry about what can happen and does happen to girls on college campuses. I don't want to contribute to the statistics.

"I promise to stick to you like glue, Mia," Kiya says, raising her right hand as if taking an oath. She isn't taking this seriously. I arch my brows, giving her a serious look.

"Let's get ready, Mia."

I acquiesce, but I'm holding her to her promise. A bar is one thing, but I've heard too many stories and most of them don't end well when it comes to college parties.

"I think I'm goo—".

Kiya interrupts me before I can finish. "Oh, no you're not. This time I choose your outfit. I don't want to be made fun of for living with the girl with the worst style ever! Plus, you owe me considering what you wore last time."

"Bu—" I start to argue, but once again my best friend cuts me off.

"No buts. Now go and shower. You look like you've been fighting a war." She couldn't be more right. I have been fighting a war—one she has no idea about.

"Fine, Mom," I tease. Still, I get up, grab my towel and head to the bathroom because arguing with Kiya is pointless. She always manages to get her way.

About an hour later, we're finally ready. And by ready, I mean R-E-A-D-Y. My hair is curled, I'm wearing my favorite high-heeled boots, which I waited two years to get from H&M. They are high but comfortable, so comfortable I can run in them if need be. I'm also wearing a gray off-the-shoulder shirt that has cuts on the sides. It shows just enough skin to be sexy, while not crossing the line. I'm also wearing skinny jeans, which I get to wear because I agreed to let Kiya do my makeup in exchange for not being forced to wear leather pants. Which brings me to the makeup. It is gorgeous—subtle, but sensual and mysterious. On a normal night, I wouldn't dream of wearing something so daring, but tonight I am feeling particularly courageous.

"Girl, you look amazing!" Kiya says. I strike a pose in response. Her eyes travel from my feet to my head. She seems pleased with her ability to make me look like a different person. She gestures to herself and waits.

I roll my eyes. "Yeah, yeah. You look great, as always." And she does. She's wearing a long-sleeved burgundy dress that falls just above the knee, paired with killer makeup and black wedges.

"Oh, shut it," Kiya replies, but I know she feels better knowing I think she looks great. She has struggled with image issues for a while, even though she's gorgeous.

"It's ten o'clock, so we can start heading there," Kiya declares.

"Okay, cool. Let me grab my purse." We exit the apartment and Kiya locks the door. It is a picturesque night. The stars light up the sky, and the temperature is perfect. Even after being in New Hampshire the whole summer, I haven't gotten used to the peaceful bright nights. I don't think I ever will.

We make our way to the party under the light of the stars. I breathe in the clean air and automatically feel at peace. There is something about this place… something that makes me feel like I can start over.

Chapter Seven

MIA

I can spot the party from a mile away. There are large groups of people congregated in different areas. They are all holding red cups, all engaged in conversation with one another. A few heads turn our way as we get near. Well, less my way and more Kiya's. She greets some people and ignores others. Some guys holler at her, calling her 'sexy' and asking when she'll let them take her out. My roommate oozes so much confidence I wish I could borrow some.

She stays by my side the whole time. I'm glad she's honoring our agreement. She also knows that I'm not good at meeting people, nor do I have any interest in meeting any of her other friends. I don't want her to feel like she has to get friends for me, or share them with me. I'll make them on my own. Eventually.

We reach the house, and the music is blasting. The front yard is full of people, and it looks like the house has vomited college students. This is the spillover. The thought of walking into a packed house makes me anxious. I want to turn around and go back home. But I push those thoughts down, and force my feet forward. Today I will be valiant, even if tomorrow I go back to being a coward.

"Are you ready for your first college party?" Kiya whispers, or attempts to whisper in my ear. She's so eager that she actually ends up yelling.

"I was expecting a small party. This one is more like a club," I whisper-yell back.

"Yeah, this is the athletes' house, so everyone wants to be at their parties. They tend to get out of control."

I eye Kiya suspiciously. Of course she would leave out this information when she asked me to come out tonight.

Kiya rolls her eyes, grabs me by the arm and shouts, "Let's go." She says something else, too, but her words are drowned out by the loud music coming from the house.

If you have ever seen any of the movies about college students and their parties, you'd be happy—or sad—to know the depictions are correct. From the moment I enter through the doors, I spot beer-pong in one corner, flip-cup in the other, very explicit dancing, and four guys rolling kegs into what I think might be the kitchen. The house is even more packed than it appeared to be from the outside. Still, I am able to make out some familiar faces, which I didn't expect to see, from my summer classes.

"Alright, you did it! You are in. Now let's go to the kitchen and get ourselves some drinks. You know what they say about alcohol," Kiya exclaims.

"Um, as a matter of fact, I have no idea what they say about alcohol. Enlighten me, genius?" I mock.

"Best social lubricant!" Kiya yells, laughing out loud and drawing attention her way.

We zigzag our way into the kitchen and grab two beers. They are canned and seem like a much safer option than the mystery punch. We pop open the cans and pour the beer into red cups.

We sip our drinks as we walk around the house. It's rather large, and we're looking for somewhere we can stand comfortably.

When we find a spot that isn't too tight, we hang out and dance to the music. I'm surprised to find that I'm truly enjoying myself.

"How are you liking it so far?" Kiya shouts over the music.

"B.U. or the party?" I ask in a similarly loud voice.

"Both."

"Well, it's not too bad. I really like the school and most of my classes so far." I pause. "And this party is fun. Thanks for forcing me to come."

"You're welcome! See, this is why you should always listen to me."

"Hmm, I'll think about that." No way am I committing to anything.

We keep dancing, our hips swinging and swaying, matching the beat. This isn't the kind of music I'm used to listening to. Back home—back in California—we'd jam to Bachata and Merengue. This isn't bad, though. Just your typical radio-crap. Still, it's good enough to dance to.

Kiya raises her red cup in the air and flips it, showing me it's empty. "I need a refill," she screams.

I look down at my cup and, disappointed at its lack of contents, look back at Kiya. She grabs my empty cup and signals to the kitchen. I nod, and she waltzes off, leaving me to guard our space.

I'm feeling more at ease now, so I don't mind being alone for a few minutes. Although a lot is happening around me, people seem too wrapped up in themselves—and each other— to pay attention to me.

Across the room, I spot a red-headed guy making his way in my direction. I look behind me, knowing it was stupid since Kiya and I had chosen a spot near the wall. I begin to panic internally.

Like legit.

I want to bolt, but I stop myself. That would clearly be overreacting and Kiya would *not let me live it down.*

I force myself to stand there as the red-head, who I eventually recognize as a guy from class—the same guy I'm in a group with, Hayes—closes the distance. He gets closer…and closer… And then he is directly in front of me. He isn't bad looking. He actually looks good.

"Hey, I'm Zack. What's your name?" he asks, his words slurring a little.

"Mia. We're in class together, remember? In the same group, actually," I say, tucking a piece of hair behind my ear—a nervous habit.

"Hey, Mia, my friend over there wants to know if he can have your number?" Zack states inches from my ear.

"Oh," I respond. I look behind him to see who he might be referring to. I spot a tall muscular guy with short blond hair.

He coughs, bringing my attention back to him. "Yeah," Then he straightens and adds, "He wants to know where he can get a hold of me in the morning."

COLTON

I hear her before I see her. Her laughter fills the room, or at least my ears, even over the sound of the music. My eyes pinpoint her in the crowd. She is bent at the waist, laughing hard at whatever Hayes has just said.

I guess she doesn't dislike everyone after all.

Just me.

Hayes is an asshole. Scratch that. A lucky asshole.

When she finally stands upright and regains her composure, her face is flushed. Zack puts his hand on her waist, edging closer to her, and whispers something else. My fingers twitch while Mia just tucks a strand of hair behind her ear.

MIA

"There's more where that came from," Zack shout-whispers in my ear.

"I bet there is," I respond, finally catching my breath after laughing so hard my sides hurt. "Do you use that line on every girl?" I ask, interested whether it usually works. Zack is as cocky as I expected him to be when I saw him sitting next to Colton in class. What I didn't expect was the cheesy pick-up line.

"If it works, why change it?" He shrugs, a smirk on his face. I bet he thinks it's swoon-worthy.

I pat him on the shoulder. "I guess you'd better go and try them on someone else, buddy."

He feigns disappointment, puts his hand on his heart, and mutters, "If you change your mind, find me." He winks and walks away.

Well, that was interesting.

I look up to find Kiya making her way back to me. With two drinks in hand, I'm afraid she'll drop my beer as she sways to the music.

Kiya hands me my cup. "Here you go."

"About time!" I exclaim. "I think I'm sober now." I give her a look of horror.

"I would've come sooner, your majesty, but you were busy with Zack." She winks at me.

I sigh. "You know red-head? Why am I not surprised?"

"Red-head? Nice nickname. Very original. And because I know everyone."

"Sarcasm, Kiya…sarcasm."

"Whatever. What was that about?" Kiya inquires, lifting her brows suggestively.

"Nothing. He wanted to test out his pick-up lines," I reply.

"Seriously?" Kiya chuckles.

"Yup."

"Aaaaand?"

"Aaaaand, nothing. I told him to go and try it on someone else."

Kiya laughs out loud. "I would've loved to have witnessed that. Way to take a shot at his ego." Kiya lifts her hand in the air and I high-five her.

"You know how I do."

The party gets bigger and louder. Kiya and I talk about class, school, and life. It's interesting how a place with so much chaos can lend itself to the deepest of conversations.

Two beers later, I get my buzz back. My body is relaxed, and not in its perpetual state of vigilance.

Not bad, Collins, not bad.

"Hey, Kiya! Come and play," a tall, handsome, dark-skinned guy yells. He is standing next to a beer pong table, the same table I had spotted when we walked into the house.

"Nah, Blake, I'm good!" Kiya responds. I know she wants to because the moment he directs the question at her, she looks like she's going to melt.

"Oh, come on. You and your friend can play. I need to beat someone new," he says cockily, walking towards us.

Kiya turns down the invitation once more.

"Alright, I understand. You're afraid you'll get your ass kicked," he says with a shit-eating grin.

Kiya rolls her eyes. "Yeah, right, that's totally why, Blake."

"We'll play," I announce, letting my competitive spirit get the better of me. Kiya turns to face me, a questioning look in her eyes. I nod in confirmation, and Kiya's eyebrows almost hit the ceiling.

"I'm game. Let's shut him up, Kiya." The words pour out of my mouth uncontrollably. Shit, I'm on fire. Talk about liquid courage.

"Alright then girls, let's play. But to make this fair, we'll do guy-girl teams."

I narrow my eyes, my feminist blood boiling. Blake thinks we have zero chance of winning, like we are doomed without a guy in our team.

"We're good. Kiya and I versus you and whoever you want," I shoot back.

Shit, what the heck am I getting myself into? My mouth and brain aren't connecting. Clearly. Kiya isn't helping either. She is watching the exchange, her gaze switching back and forth like she is watching a tennis match.

"Shit. Alright, sweetheart. Don't cry when we whoop your asses." Blake turns and approaches the table, and we follow behind him. We wait for the current game to end, and as soon as it's over, Blake requests that both teams clear the table. Well, request is putting it nicely; he shoos them away.

"Zack, come and be my partner," Blake shouts across the room "Let's show these chicks who's boss."

I cringe at the word 'chick' and the machismo display.

Clearly irritated at the interruption, Zack looks at Blake before his eyes roam over my body even though he's with another girl. He lifts his shoulders and says, "No, I'm good," then returns to his primary task of shoving his tongue down a brunette's throat. I guess I deserve that for laughing at his first attempts.

"Blake, if you're going to challenge someone and talk shit, you should at least have a partner, buddy," Kiya says, batting her eyelashes and flipping her hair in her signature Kiya-flirting move.

"I'll play," a familiar voice says from behind us. In my drunkenness, I assume I'm imagining it. I had almost made it through the whole night without thinking of him. I stand still, which is apparently my go-to move when I don't know what to do.

"Awesome. Thanks, Hunter," Blake says, confirming my

suspicions. "You girls might as well give up now," he adds while scooting closer to Kiya. She flirtatiously puts her hands on his chest and shoves him away.

While I just stand there…again.

Frozen in place.

There can be other Hunters. There *must* be.

While I convince myself that it can be a brother or a cousin, I feel the warmth of his body as he approaches us. A beautiful scent comes with it, and the smell is powerful, strong, but in the best of ways—fitting of an alpha-male.

Colton passes by me. I watch his back as he makes his way to Blake, who is standing in front of the table. But I don't just watch. I gawk. I check him out. Although dressed in the most basic of outfits, he still looks like a Greek god. Unreal.

I follow his body with my eyes. From his feet to his head. I bite my lip in admiration, and attempt to push down the feelings that are quickly rising within me. When I finally dare to look at his face, he is also biting his lip, deep in thought. Kiya nudges my shoulder, breaking me out of my trance. Thankfully, he doesn't catch me staring—again—since he seems to be strategizing with Blake. Good. The last thing I need is for him to see that he affects me in any way.

"You ready?" Kiya asks me.

"Let's do this."

Game on, bitches.

Blake sets up the cups as Colton stands there with his arms crossed, biceps straining against his t-shirt. He never once glances in my direction. If he's noticed it's me he's playing against, he doesn't show it—he probably doesn't even care.

"Alright, I assume you know how the game works, so we'll skip the introduction," Blake states. We both give him the thumps up, accompanied by an eye roll. I'm going to have too much fun kicking his ass.

"Okay, ladies, let's play!" Blake excitedly shouts. Kiya and I take our places.

"Ladies first," Blake says mockingly, dropping into a curtsey.

It makes me laugh a bit. I put my hand on Kiya's shoulder, indicating she should go first.

Kiya steps up to the plate, takes her shot and misses. By a wide margin. I see the grin on Colton and Blake's faces. Like full teeth out, triumphant smile that I oh-so-desperately want to wipe from their faces.

I take Kiya's place and hold the ping-pong ball between my thumb and index finger. I take a deep breath and take my shot. Like Kiya's, the ball skims over all the cups and bounces directly onto the floor.

The boys laugh. I say boys, because they are not men. I'm sure our rough start has made them believe this is going to be an easy win. But not tonight. What's the saying? Oh yeah, 'slow and steady wins the race', or like mami used to say, *'el que rie de ultimo rie mejor'*: This game is far from over.

Blake marches up to the table next, stretching and then fake yawns like this game is boring him. He throws the ball and it goes into one of the cups. Kiya takes the penalty, saving me by gulping down the first drink in under a minute. Next up is Colton. Instead of staring at his eyes, I look only at the ping-pong ball resting between his fingers. I look at it like it's the most interesting thing in the room. I also look at his hands. Big strong hands. Working hands maybe. He releases the ball and it bounces off the first two cups, falling into the third. I mentally curse myself and begin gulping down the beers. I finish two, while Kiya chugs the third.

I am beginning to regret my decision to play.

COLTON

Her cheeks are as red as apples. I can't tell if it's from the two beers she's just finished chugging, or something else. She's less guarded now though, and the permanent barrier she has erected has disappeared. Maybe it's the alcohol, but she seems to be, dare I say, enjoying herself. I wonder if this is the first time she doesn't give a fuck about anything or anyone around her.

I watch her once more, noting how she squints her eyes as she concentrates on the cups in front of her. She is all in, I realize, her competitive spirit taking over. She looks ready to attack. She misses her shot once more, and huffs in frustration. She's pissed. She's also hot. It's cute to see how much more pissed off she gets every time Blake and I make our shots. She really is as competitive as they get; I would recognize it anywhere.

This newfound knowledge is going to go a long way. This is my chance to get through to her. I feel as though all the stupid parties I have gone to have prepared me for this exact moment. I am going to own this game, and in doing so, hopefully get Mia's attention. If I'm honest, that's why I decided to play this game to begin with. I am drawn to her. I moved away when I saw her with Zack, but like a magnet, she's pulled me back in. Even from afar, I am aware of her every move.

I return my attention to the game; it's my turn. I concentrate as much as I can, and it helps that I'm pretty much sober. I take my shot, aiming it at the cup furthest from me, and closest to Mia. She just stands there, head bent with her right hand on her hip, staring in disbelief at the cup holding the ping pong ball.

A few minutes later, the game is over. Although the girls started doing better, Blake and I won. I can't help but smile. Mia looks mad, like she just lost an Olympic event. I fist bump Blake, grab a cup from the table and toss down the beer. When I look back up,

I see Blake making his way to the girls. I almost follow.

"I told you. No chance," I hear him say as he puts his hand on Kiya's cheek.

She is tall, dark-skinned and attractive. She smiles at Blake's gesture and shoves him playfully. I can tell she doesn't care too much about winning or losing; she just wants to flirt with him.

Mia remains behind them. She looks guarded again, her eyes roaming, taking in everything around her. She searches the room, but never looks at me.

I'm about to approach her, to get her attention once more. I crave my next fix. I take a step in her direction when I feel someone's—a girl's—arm wrap around my hips, while her chest pushes into my back. I turn around quickly and see Abby standing there. But before I can say anything, she rises onto her toes and presses her mouth against mine.

Tasting the cinnamon fireball on her lips means only one thing: she's drunk. Her hands snake into my hair. It only takes a soft sound escaping from her lips to bring me back to reality, a reality where I remember who's kissing me and what she wants. I immediately pull away, removing her hands from my hair. She looks at me, attempting a seductive smile. But I don't react. I just watch her. I don't need to remind her that we're done. She can see it in my eyes.

Her smile falls and is replaced by a pout. She realizes I'm not going to give in, so she puts her mask back on flawlessly. It's the mask she uses to hide behind. The mask that shows others that she doesn't care about being rejected. Flipping her hair, she walks away.

I stand there feeling like an asshole. I know better than to be with someone who wants more, expects more from me, yet I did it anyway. I know better than to involve myself with women. I was taught better than that by life.

The room is suddenly too full for my liking. I feel enclosed, caged, suffocated. So, I make my way to the backyard. I see Abby talking to some of her sorority sisters in the kitchen. I ignore her attempt to catch my attention again, and open the door to the backyard. I immediately feel relief. The breeze, and the stars are my haven. I sit down near the fire again. It's empty out here, everyone preferring the noise of the party to the peaceful sound of the outdoors. I put my feet on top of a stool and take a deep breath.

Chapter Eight

COLTON

I'm an idiot.

And once again I've let a woman affect me. I let her manipulate my emotions, control them. It's my fault. I need to grow up. I could have gone on with my night, but instead I let Abby piss me off, and I put myself in timeout.

Like a child.

I go back inside the house, noting that the party has not subsided. As I walk to the living room, I see a crowd gathered near the beer pong table. People are chanting loudly, cheering someone on. I move in closer to see what the commotion is all about, and that's when I see a whole row of shots lined up. In front of them are Mia and Kiya. They down shot after shot, making their way along the row while everyone hollers and yells, "Shots! Shots! Shots!"

After they are done, I see them sway on their feet, the alcohol washing too quickly through their systems. Instinctively, I want to go to Mia. I want to protect and care for her, but I also want to yell at her for being so reckless. But then I remember; she isn't mine to keep.

Like a shadow, I watch her from a distance. On shaky legs, she moves back to the dance floor, accompanied by Kiya, where they begin to dance. Their movements are sloppy, but no one is paying attention; they're all drunk too. Kiya grabs Mia's arm and spins her around in circles a couple of times. They laugh loudly, drunkenly, but also joyfully. For someone who is always so cautious, Mia's guard is down for the second time tonight. Alcohol has removed her inhibitions.

What I know for sure is that she will have no memory of this tomorrow. The only crude reminder will be a raging hangover.

She leans in close to Kiya, asking her something. Kiya lifts her hand and points in the direction of the stairs. Mia begins to move that way while Kiya's attention turns to Blake, who is calling out for her to dance. I keep my gaze on Mia as she makes her way up the stairs. That's when I see one of the guys from the hockey team, Brandon, look in her direction then follow.

I move without thinking, pushing through the massive crowd. I bump into some people on the way, but I don't give a fuck. When I get to the top of the stairs, I see Brandon make his way into a room with a blonde that appears to have been waiting for him. I'm about to head back downstairs when I see Mia stumble out of the bathroom. She's so drunk that she almost falls to the ground, but I get there fast enough to prevent her from doing a repeat of what happened in class.

She glares at me. "So, I guess this is the part where I thank you for saving me," she says mockingly, her words slurring. I don't understand what she means. Maybe this is how she acts when she's drunk.

"You don't have to do anything you don't want to do," I respond, meaning every word.

"I have manners," she retorts, leaving me confused.

Did she just imply that I have no manners?

Why is she so angry, and why is it directed at me?

"Alright, Ms. Manners, then I guess you should be thanking me. And contrary to what you may, for some unknown reason believe, I do have manners."

"Bullshit. You have no manners! You just run into people without caring about whether or not you hurt them," she says.

I flinch at her words. They are true to an extent, or at least, they had been for a while.

I used to not give a fuck about anyone else. Whoever got in my way, deserved what they got as far as I was concerned. But the way she said it, it's almost as if I've personally done something to her. That can't be the case, though. I don't remember her. I would remember her. She isn't someone you can forget, even if you tried.

"What do you mean?" I ask, running my hand through my hair.

"You ran into me and didn't bother to see if I was okay," she continues.

"What are you talking about?"

"Never mind, I'll just," she pauses, lifting her hands to make air quotes as she adds, "get over it."

She has to let me in a little tonight, even if she won't remember it tomorrow. "I don't—" I start, frustrated.

"You don't remember, do you? Of course you don't," she continues, not allowing me to speak. "I wasn't even a blip on your magnificent radar!"

"Remember what?" I ask, raising my voice. "Can you just spell it out for me?"

"Never mind," she responds as she begins to walk away. I immediately follow, taking her arm, forcing her to turn around. She looks at where I'm touching her, like she can feel the same connection to me that I feel with her—the same thing I felt the first time I touched her.

"Please, tell me," I insist softly.

"It's pointless, really. It was nothing." She flushes. "I realize that now."

"Tell me anyway," I press, because for some reason I need to know. My fingers itch to touch her again, and I give in. My hand cups her chin as I make an effort to get her to look at me. She stiffens the moment I touch her but then visibly relaxes, giving in and leaning in to me, like she too was aching to restore our connection.

"I made a big deal out of nothing. I… just forget it," she states.

"Just tell me."

She huffs. "It was two weeks ago, before classes started. My roommate and I found your sister drunk at a club, kind of like I am right now, so we called you."

Before she even finishes telling the story, it all comes back to me.

"I ran into you and told you to 'get over it', didn't I?" I say.

She nods and says, "It was pathetic. I shouldn't have made a big deal out of it, but I fell and hurt my shoulder, the least you could have done was check to see that I was okay," she says as a tear slides down her face.

"I'm sorry," I answer, feeling like the biggest asshole in the world. I can't believe I hurt her. "I'd had a really bad night. It's no excuse for my stupidity, and I'm really sorry," I say, lightly massaging both of her shoulders like that'll make it better.

"It's okay. You don't have to expl—"

"I'd just picked up my brother from jail, and then I got the call about Kaitlyn," I continue.

"I didn't know."

Of course she didn't. "Yeah, it was a shitty night, and I was in an even shittier mood. I didn't mean to run into you, and the decent thing would have been to help you up and make sure you were okay, but I had tunnel vision. I'm an asshole."

"Understandable. You don't seem like an asshole right now."

She laughs heartily, the sound of it causing me to join her.

"You say that now! And because I do actually have manners, you can call me Mr. Manners." I wink before continuing. "I apologize for my behavior." I bow, eliciting another laugh from her. I'll be damned if I'm not going to try and make her laugh as much as I can. It's music to my ears, and I want to put the sound on repeat.

"I am an occasional asshole," I add half-jokingly.

"I see that," she responds, sliding onto the floor with her back to the wall. "We didn't do our homework."

"What homework?" I ask out loud, wondering how she can change the subject so quickly.

"The questions we need to answer, and figuring out a problem. The thing we are supposed to do for Junior Seminar? You were going to text me to set up a time to meet, but you never did."

I join her on the floor. "I had a crazy day on Wednesday. Thursday wasn't much better with classes and practice, and practice again on Friday morning. I kind of slept until late Saturday," I say, internally beating myself up for forgetting to text her.

"You slept all of Friday?"

"Not all of it. I slept for like nineteen hours."

Her eyes widen. "Who the hell sleeps for that long?"

"I was exhausted." I feign a yawn, putting my hand over my mouth.

An easy silence falls between us.

"So, what do we do about the homework?" she asks shyly.

"We can do it tomorrow," I say quickly, excited at the thought of seeing her again.

She closes her eyes and leans her head on my shoulder. "Okay." We both stay like that for a while until I hear her breathing even out. I look down; she's fallen asleep.

MIA

It feels like someone is playing the drums in my head. I slowly begin to open my eyes and realize the room is dark. I turn to my left in search of my alarm clock. It isn't there. I try the other side, seeing a clock. It's six in the morning. Way too early. I pull the covers back over my head. I am not ready to start the day, not yet.

And then it hits me.

These sheets do not smell like my sheets.

These pillows are not my pillows.

My alarm clock is always on the left.

Shit.

This is not my bed.

Panic blooms and I zoom up from the bed. My heart is pounding just as loudly as my head. Disoriented, I try to get up but my feet get tangled in the sheets and I fall, face-first, on the floor.

I rise from the floor slowly, trying to regain my balance. In the near darkness, I move towards where I think the door is. I feel around on the wall for a light switch. I need to stop the darkness from consuming me. I need clarity. I need to know where I am.

I turn on the light, and look around. This is definitely not my room. I see a mirror and go to it. I want to look at myself, to make sure I'm okay. I look at my reflection, and aside from the makeup that covers my face, everything seems okay. Biting my lip, I look down to find I'm still wearing the clothes I had on the night before. Relief swamps me. I was not attacked, or at least there is no sign of it. Still, the lingering question is, where am I? And why am I sleeping in someone else's room? I walk back towards the door, but stop dead in my tracks when it opens…

And Colton walks in.

Sweat is dripping from his forehead, running down his face and into the neck of his gray muscle shirt. Judging by his shoes, he's just come back from a run, but who the hell runs at six in the morning? And then it hits me.

I'm in *his* room.

The pit in my stomach becomes a massive sinkhole and I want it to swallow me whole.

"How the hell did I end up here?" I ask him, afraid of what the answer might be.

"You don't remember what happened last night?" he asks with a smirk.

I remember pieces of it, like how we were playing beer pong, how I saw him kissing the blonde, how it had made me feel when he'd followed her. Something resembling jealousy had risen deep within my stomach, but knowing it wasn't mine to feel, I pushed it down the only way I knew how—the only way my father knew—with alcohol.

Salt. Tequila. Lime. Repeat.

"I don't…Why am I here? Is this your room?" Internally, I am in full panic mode. Externally, though, I'm keeping it together. I need all the missing pieces from last night. I need to know why I woke up in this room, in his room. Kiya and I were supposed to stick together. Where is she?

"She stayed with Blake," Colton says before I even formulate the question, like he can read my mind.

Kiya likes Blake, I know that. I'm sure she'll be safe with him, but I'm hurt that she left me. We had an agreement.

"She's still in the house. You were both too drunk to go home. So, Blake offered for you both to stay here. Blake took her in, and I took you in," he says calmly. He moves from the door and leans on his desk, arms crossed, sweat still dripping. I fight the urge to lick my lips.

"Why not just leave us in the same room? Why separate us? Don't you think it's a little weird to take a girl you don't know into your room? Where did you sleep?"

The questions come out too fast, my mind going a million miles per hour.

"Wouldn't be the first time," he responds.

Asshole.

"And where do you think I slept?" he asks.

"I'm not in the mood to play games, Colton. Since you remember what happened last night, tell me."

He finally realizes I'm not joking. Sitting on the chair in front of his desk, he turns to me and says, "Okay. I was outside getting some fresh air. When I came back inside, you and Kiya were doing shots. Then you went upstairs to the bathroom, I think. I happened to be up there because I was going to talk to one of the guys. You came out of the bathroom, tripped and almost fell. I caught you and we sat on the floor for a bit. I stayed with you because I wanted to make sure you were alright."

As he talks, things start coming back to me. I recall feeling like the rug had been pulled out from under me. I remember falling, and then someone holding me.

"What happened after you caught me?" I ask, trying to get the full picture.

"We talked about how much of an ass I was to you when we first met. I apologized and you, Ms. Manners, fell asleep on my shoulder."

Hearing him tell me what happened brings the rest of the memories back. I remember him sitting next to me on the floor while I leaned on his shoulder with my eyes closed.

"Where did you sleep?"

"I slept on the couch." I follow his pointing finger toward the other end of the room. I see the messy sheets on top of the couch. Relief spreads through me once again. I didn't sleep with anyone last night. I didn't sleep with him. I just slept.

"Oh, okay. Well, thank you for letting me stay the night," I state, bouncing on my toes. Ready to go, yet somehow still standing in the same place.

"Yeah, anytime." He scratches his head. "And, hey, be careful when you're drinking, okay? You know, this world is full of assholes willing to take advantage of anyone they can." His sentiment seems honest and sincere. But he isn't telling me anything I don't know. I have encountered too many assholes in my lifetime already. Until recently, he was among them.

"Wait, isn't your girlfriend going to be pissed that you let another girl spend the night?" I ask the moment I remember the girl he had been making out with last night.

"If this is your way of asking me if I'm single, the answer is yes," he teases.

"No, this is my way of asking if the girl you were making out with last night would mind," I reply before I can censor myself. I feel the jealousy dripping from my words as the statement leaves my mouth. I hope he doesn't notice.

"She might, but it doesn't matter. She and I are nothing," he says matter-of-factly.

"Seemed like more than nothing last night," I counter. Why the hell am I going down this rabbit hole? It's none of my business. "Never mind; it's none of my business," I repeat out loud. Wanting him to know I couldn't care less. "I'm going to go." I walk towards the door, but spin on my heel when he takes hold of my arm.

"Where are you going?"

"Home," I say, "It's not common practice for me to stay in a stranger's room."

He frowns. "It's six in the morning. You're going to walk home at this time?" he asks.

"Why not?"

His eyes travel over my body. "Because you'll look like you're doing the walk of shame."

My eyes get as big as saucers. I didn't think about what I would look like walking out of this room in the same clothes as last night.

"If I leave later, it'll be the same, plus the entire house will be up by then. The best option is to leave now when the least number of people will notice." I reach for the doorknob once again.

"Just...wait." He begins to look through his drawers. "Let me get you some clothes so you can change out of that outfit." He pulls out a black hoodie and some sweatpants, and hands them to me.

I stare at him, wondering if he wears anything other than sweats, hoodies, and muscle shirts.

"Okay. Thanks." I eye him intently. When he doesn't get the clue, I raise my eyebrows and say, "Would you mind? I'm not about to give you a show by changing in front of you."

His eyes widen. "Shit! Yeah, I'll... um... I'll leave." He trips on the chair as he begins walking towards a door. "Let me grab my towel and I'll take a quick shower while you change. Then I can give you a ride home."

"You don't have to. I can walk. It's not that far."

"I want to," he replies. "Plus, we've got homework to do, Ms. Manners"

He remembered. "That nickname is already annoying."

"You can always call me Mr. Manners," he says as he disappears into the bathroom, closing the door behind him. Within seconds, the shower turns on. Taking advantage of being alone, I peruse his room. My initial inspection shows that aside from the mess of sheets on the couch and the bed, the room is spotless.

Still holding on to the clothes, I move toward the bookcase

across from the couch. I move quickly through the book titles and my attention is captured when I find some of my favorites: Emily Bronte's Wuthering Heights, Zora Neal Hurston's Their Eyes Were Watching God, and Octavia E. Butler's Kindred. Feeling like I've snooped for far too long, I change into the clothes Colton gave me. While changing, I keep an eye on the bathroom door, afraid it'll open, and I'll be exposed. The sweatshirt he lends me is down to my thighs, and the sweatpants are way too big. I roll them up at the waist until I look semi-normal and they are no longer dragging on the floor. Then I hear the water shut off. Seconds later, the door opens. Colton comes out with a towel wrapped around his hips. Every muscle is visible. I lick my lips at the sight of his six pack and the V disappearing under the edge of his towel.

"Fuck, sorry. I forgot to grab my clothes," he says sheepishly.

"Ah," I clear my throat and try again. "No problem. I'll be… I have to go to the bathroom anyway." I walk around him closing the door behind me.

Come on, Mia. Pull yourself together.

Chapter Nine

MIA

"Kiya is staying for a little longer," Colton tells me closing the door to the house behind him.

"Of course she is." I roll my eyes. Typical Kiya.

"Blake will take her home later," he says, "He's a good guy," he adds sensing my hesitation.

He walks toward the passenger side of his Camaro and opens the door for me. This car is still as hot as hell. I remember it from the night at Eclipse, but somehow it looks a lot better today.

"Are you going to get in or just continue checking me out?" Colton says, lifting an eyebrow.

"I… Me? Wait. I wasn't checking you out," I respond.

"Am I supposed to believe you were checking out Lex?"

I look around to see if anyone else has joined us. "Who's Lex?"

"Alexa over here," he states, pointing at the car.

I laugh. "You named your car Alexa, and nicknamed it Lex?"

"Everyone names their car. Now stop avoiding the inevitable and fess up to checking me out."

"I'm checking out something alright. But it isn't you. Is this the 1969 Camaro SS?" I ask, running my fingers along the hood of the car.

"Ah, yes," he says, confused.

"Automatic or standard transmission?"

"Standard."

"Is it true what they say?"

He winks. "It depends on what they're saying."

"Does it go from zero to sixty in three point five seconds?" I like speed, maybe a little too much and it's probably because of my obsession with the Fast and Furious Franchise.

"Yeah… it does," he responds with a surprised look in his eyes.

"What?" I ask, shifting my eyes from him to the gorgeous machine in front of me.

"I'm just a little surprised you know about cars."

I scoff. "Because I'm a girl?"

"If I say yes, does that make me sexist?"

"Maybe a little. I'll have you know I also do—did—my own oil changes and changed my own tires," I counter, attempting to hide the smile that is slowly spreading across my face.

"Then nope, not at all because you're a girl. More like because you're the only girl to ever ask," he says finding a loophole in my logic. I slide into the passenger seat. He closes my door and jogs over to the driver's side. Seconds later, we're on the road.

"So where do you live?" he asks me.

"Hmm, you can just leave me at the fitness center."

"Are you working out?" he asks with a giant smile on his face.

I smile back. "No, but it's close enough to my house."

"How about you just tell me your address and I'll take you home. I promise I won't stalk you."

"That's exactly what a stalker would say," I say only half-jokingly.

"You're probably right. But hey, you know where I live. It's only fair."

"Not by choice. It's not like I wanted to show up at your house. I was dragged there."

"I don't think you minded it too much. I mean most girls would die to say they spent the night."

"I'm sure they would, but not me. You're not really my type."

He chuckles. "Really?"

Damn that chuckle.

"Yeah, and neither are one-night stands or hookups. So, get your mind out of the gutter!"

"Love, I said 'spent the night', as in slept over. I think the only mind in the gutter is yours. Now, would you mind telling me where you live?"

I flush.

I tell him my address and he proceeds in the direction of my home.

I watch him as he drives. He's got one hand on the steering wheel and the other on the gearshift. My eyes carry on with their journey upward. His amazing broad shoulders. Damn, even his jaw is attractive. I look at his lips and see that he's biting down a smile.

"What are you smiling at?" I ask, unable to stop myself.

"I can literally feel you checking me out." He chuckles, keeping his eyes on the road.

"I am not!" I scoff.

"Sure you aren't. Totally *not* checking me out like your favorite library book."

"Library book? Really?" I say.

He briefly glances in my direction before fixing his eyes back on the road. "What?"

"Nothing. It's just funny. You could have said 'check out like groceries', or something else, but nope, you chose books. That was totally unexpected."

He sighs loudly. "Whatever." His tone is terse and I think I may have offended him. I sit quietly in my seat, afraid to say anything else.

"So, Maya, we need to do the assignment today."

I turn in his direction. "It's Mi—" I stop when I see the amusement dancing in his eyes.

The asshole did it on purpose.

I guess it's fair since I insulted his intelligence.

"You are the worst!" I laugh. This might be the first time someone messes up my name just to tease me. I watch him bite his lip, trying to contain his laughter.

"That's what you get for typifying me as a dumb jock." I'm about to apologize when he continues, "But seriously, where do you want to do this?"

"Do what?" I ask, feeling a little lost.

"The assignment, woman!"

"Oh, that. Hmm, don't we need to figure out when Zack is available?"

"Zack is out of commission for the day. He's nursing a major hangover," he states, pulling into my driveway.

"So, he's the type that blows off homework?" I ask, trying to prove my theory that there's at least one slacker in every group.

"He'll catch up. So, are we doing this?" he asks again.

"I have to take a shower and change," I blurt out.

"Okay, is that an invitation to join you? Because I already showered today." As he says this, I feel my cheeks warm.

"No!" I shove him.

"So then, back to the original question. Where do we do it?"

Because I'm not a morning person, and because I have a hangover, I can't really think right now. "Let me get ready and then we can figure it out," I reply.

"Okay, so I'll wait for you then."

"Wait, you want do it right now?"

"I thought you said after you shower?"

"Yeah, well, I thought that you meant later. Don't you have

stuff to do?"

"Yeah, it's called homework."

"Homework you weren't too interested in doing on Friday, huh?"

Teasing him comes so naturally; it's like we've been doing it for years.

"On Friday I had practice and then I slept like a hibernating bear."

Maybe it won't be so bad to spend a little more time with him. We do have to finish this part of the assignment by tonight. "Okay, I'll shower and then we can go somewhere." I start walking towards my apartment when I feel him behind me. I turn around quickly and he stops in his tracks.

"What's up?" he asks, concern etched on his face.

"Oh, um, I don't really let strangers into my house," I say hesitantly.

"Me?" He points at himself. "I'm a stranger? Unbelievable," he says with a grin.

"Yes, you are," I answer, glad he doesn't take it the wrong way.

"But you've already slept with me!" he whines.

"I did no such thing! I slept over, and not by choice. Huge difference," I reply.

"It's okay. I'm only busting your b— Giving you a hard time. I think it's good to protect yourself. I'll wait out in the car," he responds.

"But what if I take two hours to get ready?"

"Then you might have to wake me up from the nap I'll be taking in Alexa."

"That sounds really weird. Maybe you shouldn't have named your car," I joke.

"Ha, ha, very funny! Now go and shower. We have work to do."

I almost stop him and tell him it's okay for him to come inside, but I think better of it. That is not something I do, and I'm not about to let him throw my norms out the window. Even though, in a way, he already has.

COLTON

Here I am, sitting in the car with the seat reclined, listening to Michael Jackson. Well, it's more like Michael Jackson is playing in the background because I can't stop my mind from looping the question of 'what am I doing here?' And I don't mean just here inside my car, or even here waiting for Mia, but just here with Mia overall. Because I know what I'm not doing with her. She slept in my bed, but not with me. She woke up in my room this morning, and didn't just sneak out in the middle of the night. She got ready in my bathroom, and then I volunteered to drive her home. And now? Now I'm waiting for her outside her house. Like she means something.

Like she means something to me.

The thought of turning on the car and peeling out of her driveway briefly crosses my mind, but it's soon overpowered by the memory of her sleeping in my bed. How peaceful and beautiful she'd looked with one leg over the blanket, her hair all over her face, and one arm hugging a pillow.

Even her snoring was a comforting sound. And then I realized regardless of how beautiful and innocent she might seem, she could also be deceiving and spiteful too.

Because that's how women are.

Because that's how my—

My thoughts are interrupted when I see Mia come out of the house, shutting the door behind her.

She walks to my car slowly, unsure if she should be here. That makes two of us.

Opening up the passenger door, she slides inside.

"So?" she says as she puts on her seatbelt.

"So?" I repeat.

"Where are we doing this?"

"Where do *you* want to do this, Mia?" I ask, lifting an eyebrow suggestively.

Chapter Ten

MIA

I didn't really expect him to be sitting in his car by the time I got out. Part of me hoped he'd left while I was in the shower. Today has been embarrassing enough. I wonder why he stayed, though. Why did he take me in, drive me home, and wait for me? He probably did it for Blake, so that he could spend more time alone with Kiya. Maybe he's not as shitty a person as I think he is.

"—Mia?"

Crap. "What?" I ask, hoping my blush doesn't show.

"Wow, you either haven't fully woken up or you're still checking me out."

"I haven't had my coffee," I say, ignoring his second comment.

"Okay, so let's get you some." I feel my eyebrows bunch up at his response. "Some coffee," he adds and smiles. A really contagious smile that has me smiling back.

"Yeah, coffee. Sorry, I'm not me when I'm caffeine deprived."

"Did you just remake the Snickers commercial?"

"Maybe, or maybe they remade my coffee commercial."

"Yeah that's probably the more likely scenario."

"So, coffee?" I say.

"Yeah, I know just the place. You can go back to being human and we can actually get started on the homework all at the same time."

"Works for me."

The car ride is quiet. I spend it looking down at my hands, or out the window watching the trees go by. I look up when the car comes to a stop in front of something that looks like a trailer truck, but has a sign with the words West Side Diner on top of it. From the outside, it looks like the place belongs in the early 1950s. My door opens, and I look down to find Colton holding out his hand to me. After a moment's hesitation, I take it, feeling the sparks on contact.

I step out of the car. "Wow, you really take the door thing seriously? Afraid I'm going to slam it?" I mock, taking my hand back and immediately feeling the emptiness.

"I told you, I actually have manners. This isn't a façade I'm putting up just for you."

"If you say so."

"I do."

"So, West Side Diner? Feeling like Grease?" I respond.

"It's actually a pretty cool place. I come here for breakfast every Sunday."

"Look at you, sharing your most prized possessions with me. First your bed, then your car, and now your diner. What's next?"

I don't know where I'm going with this, but I can't stop myself from saying it anyway.

"You'll have to stick with me to find out." Sticking with him doesn't sound like the worst idea. Still, I better not get used to it.

"So, are we going to go inside or just watch it from here?" I say instead, ignoring his comment.

"Very funny. Let's go."

Inside the diner, it's more old school than I would have imagined. The booths are red and white, matching the waiters' striped uniforms. Very fun, very retro, and very busy it seems. The crowd is different from what I'm used to at the college coffee shop. This one is full of older people. No college students in sight, aside from Colton and me.

A really beautiful middle-aged waitress greets us with a warm smile and gives Colton a hug before leading us to a booth.

"Do you want the usual, Colton?" she asks him as she hands me a menu.

She knows his name? Maybe he does come here all the time. It does make me wonder if I'm the first girl he's brought here though. Would they think I'm just another notch on his bedpost?

He smiles at her. "Yes, please, Karla."

"And for you?" she asks, turning her attention to me.

"Coffee, please." She nods then leaves. "What's the usual?" I ask Colton.

He grins. "French toast, pancakes, eggs, bacon, home fries and two glasses of orange juice."

"Are we feeding a small country?"

"Yeah, they all live inside my body and I have to make sure I keep them alive."

"Well, I certainly was not expecting that response," I say, laughing.

"You asked. Never ask a question you don't want the answer to."

"I— Okay." My coffee arrives and after smelling the deliciousness, I take a sip; my mood instantly lifts.

"Okay, let's start. Do you have the sheet with the instructions and the getting to know you questions?" I ask, ready to take on the world now that I've had my caffeine.

"No, I left it at home."

"Seriously?"

"No, Mia, of course not. I have it here." He pulls it out of the back pocket of his jeans, placing the slightly crumpled folded paper on top of the table.

"Let me read the instructions."

He passes the paper to me, adding, "Just read them out loud. I haven't had a chance to look at them yet."

"Okay." I unfold the paper and begin to read. "The homework is divided into parts. First, on the next page of this packet, you will find a series of questions that every person in your group must answer in full. In answering these questions, the group will find issues that are important to each of you.

This will facilitate part two of the assignment, where you will need to select a world problem you'd like to fix. Once the problem is selected, you cannot change it. You may also not change the group you are a part of. There will be subsequent assignments, but for Monday's class, you will need to submit the answers to the questions and a statement of the problem you will try and fix along with the reason you have chosen it.

As I mentioned before, this is a humanities course, and the purpose of it is to make you look outside of your immediate surroundings, find an issue that interests you, and work on figuring out a solution. This is due on Monday during class, and if not received at the beginning of class you will lose fifteen percent of the final project grade."

I finish reading the instructions, thinking about what could have happened to my final grade if we didn't work on the assignment.

"Sounds like we're superheroes who need to play the marriage game before saving the world," Colton says, and I almost spit out my coffee.

"How Well Do You Know Your Spouse?" I add, wondering if that's the game he's referring to.

"Yeah, that one."

"I hate that game. It gives the illusion that the people committing to each other know their partner well. When in actuality, no one really knows anyone well."

"You can say that again," he says so softly I almost miss it.

"Okay, what's the first question?"

"Which do you prefer, cats or dogs?" I read out loud.

"Dogs."

"Cats."

We answer at the same time. I'm a little confused as to how this will help us figure out a world issue. Maybe the professor thinks we're going to do something about animals in crisis.

"Why dogs?" I ask though it's not relevant.

"Because they're fun, playful, and I can take them out for runs. Why cats, Cat Lady?"

"Because they're independent, not needy, and don't give a crap about people—something I aspire to."

"Well, this is going to be a long day. Next question."

"Okay, so you prefer dogs over cats, your favorite article of clothing is jackets, and your favorite holiday is Christmas," I say to Colton, who is busy feasting on the insurmountable amount of food he ordered. He's finished his pancakes, and is starting on his eggs. He passed the French toast to me a few minutes after getting his meal because he thinks he won't finish it, and thinks I need to eat something. Apparently, coffee doesn't count as a meal.

Although I initially refuse, I take him up on the offer because I'm still nursing a hangover, and it'll get better if I have real food in my stomach.

"It's not like your answers are any better: cat lady, boots, and Thanksgiving."

"Are you badmouthing Thanksgiving?"

"Ah, what's so great about it?" he asks.

"Food!" I reply enthusiastically.

"There's food for Christmas, too."

"Yeah, but there are presents and whatnot which take away from the holiday."

"But you still have food."

"Yes, but there's just too much going on. Thanksgiving is all about giving thanks and eating."

"Okay, okay. I guess that's passable. Next question," he says.

"When was the last time you climbed a tree?"

"What the…? These questions are really weird and not at all helpful in determining a topic. The last time I climbed a tree was in camp when I was about seven years old."

"Wow, you have not had much of a life."

"When was the last time you climbed a tree, adventurer?"

"I climbed a tree when I was a senior in high school. My mom, my dad, and I went back home to the Dominican Republic and I climbed a tree to get some mangoes."

He looks impressed. "Wow, that's quite a story. Next time I'm in a Caribbean country, remind me to give you a call."

"Ha ha, very funny. I'm not climbing a tree for you. Get your own mangoes." I pop a home fry in my mouth and look at him, challenging him to say something else.

He finishes a spoonful of eggs, but otherwise keeps his mouth shut.

We continue to go back and forth with a few more questions. I laugh at some of his ridiculous answers, like the fact that his weirdest crush is Simon Cowell from the X-Factor.

"Why the heck do you like him? He's so mean!"

"Well, he tells it like it is. He doesn't bullshit. He's honest. He doesn't deceive. And if you don't have it, he'll tell you to your face. I guess I've always liked the fact that Simon stabs you in the face, never in the back."

"Okay," I respond. Not quite sure what else to say. I clear my throat and move on to the next question. We get through nine of the ten questions the professor has on the list.

"Okay, the last question is, what is something you've read or seen recently that has made you upset or angry?"

"I read a social media post from a guy at another school boasting about a girl he'd purposefully gotten drunk so she'd sleep with him. I hate it when people take advantage of others that are unable to stand up for themselves," Colton responds. I'm left speechless, remembering the guys surrounding Colton's sister the week before.

"I agree. I think people taking advantage of others is what pisses me off the most."

"Okay, so if we had to choose a problem, what would it be?" he asks.

"Um, that's not part of the list of questions."

"Nope, but that's the purpose of the questions, and considering we have to hand this in tomorrow, we might as well choose a problem."

"Okay, well what about something related to sexual assault?" I suggest uncomfortably.

"Sexual assault affecting a vulnerable population? Remember, we have to be global."

"Yeah, so I know sexual assault is a giant issue on college campuses, but globally I'd have to say human sex trafficking."

"Why don't we narrow it down to child sex trafficking?"

"God, now that's a problem I'd like to solve."

"You and me both. Fuck people that take advantage of others. But fuck them even more if they take advantage of kids."

I don't add anything to his statement. I don't feel like I need to. "Should we run it by Zack to see if he agrees?" I ask.

"No, he's not here. He'll have to suck it up," he states matter-of-factly.

"Well, that's that. I know more about you than I wanted to know, but it all led to the choosing of a good topic," I say half-jokingly, trying to drag us back from the dark direction our conversation had just taken.

"Oh, shut it, you know you've always wanted to know my favorite colors, the last thing I Googled, and if I sing in the shower."

"You'd like to think that now, wouldn't you? Plus, I already know you don't sing in the shower. Remember? I slept with you last night."

Shit. I did *not* mean for that to come out the way it did.

"Maybe I was repressing my soul's song for fear that you'd be more frightened than you were when I walked into the room the first time. Also, I'm glad you've admitted to sleeping with me."

I chuckle and throw a fry at him. "Shut up! You know what I mean."

"We should probably finish up here," he says.

"We should, I have some things to do, and I'm sure you do too, so let's get the check."

"Alright, yeah. I meant we should leave the diner because we've been sitting here for a few hours now and I don't want to make my favorite waitress mad at me because she isn't getting tips from other customers since we're hogging her table."

"Right." I definitely thought he just wanted to abandon ship.

"I was going to suggest we go somewhere else, but I know you have plans, and we're done with the first part of the assignment, so..."

"Plans? What plans?" I ask.

"I thought you said you have some things to do."

"Oh, those things. Really important things. I should definitely get to it."

"I'll drop you off," he says. Maybe it's for the better that we cut our time short. The next thing you know, I'll be getting used to having someone other than Kiya to hang out with. It's dangerous, but not as dangerous as getting close to someone who will eventually leave me.

Colton makes eye contact with the waitress and three minutes later the check arrives.

"I'll get it," we both respond in unison.

"Let me get it." I like to pick up the tab. I don't want anyone to get the idea that I owe them anything.

"No, you don't have to do that," he counters, holding on to the check and pulling it in his direction.

"Why, because I'm a woman and men have to pay? Will you feel emasculated if I pick up the tab?"

"Um no, because I ordered a shit ton of food and you only got coffee so it wouldn't be fair for you to pay when you didn't order as much."

Fair point. "Oh, well… I also had French toast," I argue pathetically.

"Yes, and again in the grand scheme of things, I ordered it. Even if you had, it still makes it two items to fifteen."

"You didn't get fifteen things."

"Will you just let me pay?" he says, sounding a little annoyed.

"Okay," I concede. "But let me at least get the tip."

"You won't let it rest, will you?"

"I don't like feeling like I owe people."

"I wouldn't ask you to pay me back. Plus, if you pay, I'd be owing you. I don't want to owe you."

"Alright. I'll get the tip, you get the check."

"I'll get everything this time, and you can get everything next time."

"Next time?" His words light up a tiny match of hope within me. There will be a next time. He wants to hang out with me again.

"Yeah, we have to work together to finish this project. You're stuck with me for the rest of the semester."

Oh yeah, I forgot. The only reason he's even here with me is homework, but even knowing that, I can't help but smile.

Chapter Eleven

MIA

Our ride back from the restaurant is probably a little worse than our drive to it. We don't talk much and I don't really think he wants to, so I stay quiet too. With a quiet "goodbye", I open up the front door and shut it behind me, letting out a deep sigh of relief.

Thank God that's over.

"You're back! Where have you been?" Kiya practically screams when she comes out of her bedroom.

"Doing homework," I say nonchalantly. Like it isn't a big deal, because it isn't.

"Considering I just saw Colton pull out the driveway, I want to know what kind of homework you were doing," she says with a wicked grin.

"I'll have you know we were working on our group project."

"What group project?" Kiya asks, and I remember I haven't told her I'm in a class with Colton.

"We're taking Junior Seminar together," I respond while keeping my eyes down. I'd do anything to avoid the look I know she's giving me right now for not telling her.

"You have a class with Colton?" she squeaks excitedly. She

starts jumping up and down like a child hopped up on sugar. "Why didn't you tell me?"

I gesture at her. "Do you have to ask?"

Once I get through her cross-examination about my whereabouts and my class with Colton, I start on her. She did stay with Blake after the party, and with a little pressure, she tells me she shared his bed.

"But nothing more happened," Kiya insists.

"Really?"

"I mean, I like him—obviously. I've been crushing on him for a year now, but I refuse to act on it."

"Why?"

"Blake has a reputation of not committing to one girl. Plus, he has a tendency to get into trouble. But the thing is, he texts me every day, and he's always at whatever party I'm at. He even tells me he's 'feeling me' every time he sees me."

"And?" I prompt when she hesitates.

She shrugs. "It's not enough. If he's only after one thing, he won't be getting it from me."

I'm actually proud of her for not giving in.

"Are you hungry?" Kiya asks, artfully changing the subject. She walks into the kitchen and takes some chicken from the fridge.

I nod and sigh. "What am I going to do without you when you leave?"

"For starters, starve," she responds, adding seasoning to the meat.

"You can say that again. Would you mind teaching me?"

"How much time do we have?"

"Funny," I deadpan. "I'm a quick learner."

"Yeah, you learn what you want to learn really quickly. How will you feed your husband?"

"I don't want to learn for a husband. I'm more concerned with how

I'll feed myself."

"My family says unless you know how to cook, you can't get married."

"Seriously? My grandfather used to say the same thing. Mom, too."

"Yet you never learned?" she says as she turns on the oven.

"Well, I'd like to believe my husband will cook for the both of us. Plus, I don't subscribe to these roles. Why do I have to cook? Can't I just be the bread-winner?"

"Equality means you both learn, Mia."

"Yeah, yeah. Anyway, speaking of food, when will it be ready? I'm starving," I say.

"Didn't you have food at the diner?" she asks like she just caught me in a lie.

"Barely. I had coffee. And a little bit of Colton's food, but not enough to fill me up; my stomach wasn't up for it."

"Aw, you guys shared food and everything. You withheld important information from me, Mia!"

"How's that important? And, no, we didn't share food. He didn't feed it to me, Ki. He ordered too much and told me to eat some."

"Sharing his bed, now his food. I wonder what else you'll be sharing." She hip-checks me while wiggling her eyebrows.

"And you wonder why I didn't tell you I have class with him," I mutter under my breath, but still loud enough for her to hear.

"Don't remind me of your indiscretion. I should just make food for myself to punish you."

"I should stop being your friend for getting super drunk and leaving me alone at his house," I retort.

Kiya's smile fades. "I'm so sorry about that, Mia."

"I was joking."

"No, you're not. I messed up. I had one job."

And we're back to this conversation.

"Kiya, its ok—"

"No, it's not, Mia. I made you go to the party with me. I knew how you felt about them. And instead of making sure we weren't separated, and that one of us was sober enough to get the two of us home, I got plastered. And, well, you woke up in a stranger's room. I'm so sorry. I am a terrible friend." Her eyes are watering now.

"No, Kiya," I begin, immediately feeling guilty for putting so much pressure on her. "I chose to go to that party. You asked me to go with you, but I made the decision. It wasn't your job to keep me safe. We both got too drunk. I somehow ended up upstairs talking to Colton. Blake assured you it would be okay. And although Blake may be a lot of things, you think he's a good person. We couldn't drive back home, and although it would have made more sense to stay in the same room, you knew nothing bad would happen to me."

"I will not pressure you to go to any more parties. Shoot, I think it would do me well to not go to any either."

"I probably won't be going to any anytime soon. But you," I point at her and in the most dramatic way I can, I add, "I'd love to see the day you turn down a party."

"Shut up! I can be a homebody." She puts the chicken in the oven.

"I have to work hard and play harder," I say, mocking my roommates' earlier words.

"Will you ever let that go?"

"Nope. Anyway, you should still have fun. I had fun."

"You did?" She grabs a pot from the bottom cabinet and starts to fill it with water.

"Yeah, I loved that you and I got to just talk, and for a moment, I was able to let loose and enjoy myself. Drinking was fun, dancing in the middle of the dance floor was exciting. Playing beer pong was cool, though if I ever do that again, you will not be my partner."

"Me?" she gasps. "But I was wonderful. *You sucked."*

I laugh. "That's not how I remember it; we both sucked."

"Maybe it's for the better we never team up," Kiya says while measuring the rice and adding it to a plastic bowl.

"Agreed," I state, watching my roommate wash the rice. I'd seriously die of hunger without her.

"Anyway, even the short conversation with Hayes was fun. And even more surprisingly, I had a decent conversation with Colton."

"Did you now?" she asks.

"Well, it must have been an okay conversation considering I fell asleep."

"That's probably the first time that's ever happened to him."

I don't doubt it. I'm sure most girls hang on his every word.

"When I realized you hadn't come back, I went up to check on you, to see if you needed me to hold back your hair," Kiya says.

"You did?" I ask, remembering how the two of us held back Kaitlyn's hair weeks before.

"I saw Colton come down from the stairs and asked him if he'd seen you."

"You expected him to know who I was?"

"I described you as the girl who had lost terribly to him at beer pong," she laughs

"Very funny!"

"He told me you fell asleep in the hallway and he took you up to a room."

"That sounds real creepy."

"I thought so too, but he showed me what room you were in. I saw you passed out on a bed, fully clothed. He assured me you'd be okay and that no one would come into the room."

"Well, he lied because he slept there."

"No, he didn't."

"Yes, he did. He told me he slept on the couch. I saw the sheets there."

"That's odd," Kiya says. "No, he slept in the room next door to Blake's. It was empty because they had kicked out one of the athletes last month for 'questionable behavior'." She says the last part making air quotes.

"If that was the case, why not put me in that room?"

"He said no one would go into the room you were in because it was his."

I am relieved by her words. I feel a sense of gratitude towards Colton for trying to make sure nothing bad happened to me. I also feel like kicking him in the shins for making me think we shared a room.

"He told me he slept on the couch."

"He was probably just trying to see how you'd react. Busting your chops."

"I want to bust his chops," I mutter before thinking about how that sounds coming out of my mouth.

"More like jump his bones," Kiya responds. I roll my eyes and start setting up the table.

Like clockwork, Monday arrives.

Yes, Monday from hell, where my alarm clock sounds like an ambulance, firetruck, and ice cream truck all at the same time.

I stop whining and turn to my right, smacking the clock and making it stop.

It has once again done its job because I am awake.

I run through my morning routine, and get a coffee from the student café. I arrive to class fifteen minutes early, and I'm about to take a seat, when I remember I now have a new one. Because I'm in a group that sits in the back. I can't even see too well from there, but that's where I'm stuck.

I sit down and briefly consider switching my seat to take the one next to Colton instead of Zack, but think better of it; I don't think Colton and I are actually friends now.

I distract myself by playing on my phone again. A few minutes later I look up to see Colton making his way towards me. I lick my lips instinctively. His hair is still wet, and my fingers itch to run through it. He's wearing a flannel shirt, which does a bad job of hiding his bulging biceps, and jeans. I suddenly wish I was back at my regular seat, so I can take a look at his likely glorious ass. He reaches the top of the stairs and takes Zack's seat. I glance around the room, seeing it's still relatively empty.

Why is he here so early?

He pulls out a binder and begins studying it intently.

I want to say hello because it seems like the reasonable thing to do considering I spent a large part of yesterday and the night before with him, but I'm afraid. What if he ignores me like he did the other girl?

In the end, I decide to woman up and speak first.

"Hey," I say, my voice a little shaky.

His piercing gray eyes meet mine. My breath stops and I can physically feel the weight of his gaze. If I wasn't already sitting down, I'd have likely fallen judging by the way my knees are shaking. I wait, wondering what will happen next. Will he dismiss me or acknowledge me?

"Hi."

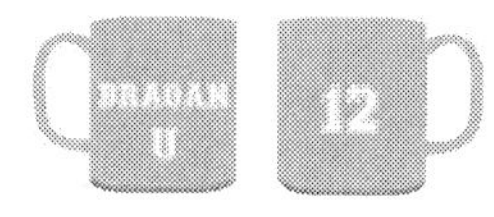

Chapter Twelve

COLTON

Hi? Is that the only thing I can say back?

Yesterday was so easy with her, so refreshing. Not once did she flirt with me. Not once did she act like all the other girls in my class. She looks like she's about to say something else, but thinks better of it as she sees the class fill up. I curse myself for not finding more words to say to her to prolong our conversation.

"Okay class," I hear the professor say from the front of the room. "Settle down, settle down. Find your seats." Everyone starts to quiet down. "Okay, I hope you've all spent the last few days figuring out your topic. Let's have someone from each group share the issue they came up with to make sure no one is solving the same world problem." He glances around the room, zeroing in on me and Mia. "Ms. Collins and Mr. Hunter, it appears that the third member of your trio is absent today."

"Sick with the stomach bug," I respond without thinking, covering for Zach on autopilot.

"Of course he is," he replies drily before moving on. "Okay, group one, tell us what you'll be fixing?"

A short redheaded girl stands up and says, "My group wants to focus on access to clean water."

"Wonderful! Water is crucial to life. Did anyone else think of the same topic?"

A group a few rows from us raise their hands.

"You will need to pick out a new problem. Water is already taken." A collective groan fills the room. I hope no one else has chosen our topic, not that I think they will because not too many college students think of child sex trafficking as a problem that still exists.

The professor goes from group to group and minutes later, Abby stands from her chair to present hers.

"We will be talking about sexual education." She turns to look in my direction and winks as the class laughs.

"Ms. Brown, how does this fit with the assignment?"

"Well, easy Prof, the world needs sex education to prevent the spread of sexually transmitted diseases, unwanted pregnancies and so on."

"Great. Moving onto the duo."

I look at Mia, waiting to see if she's going to stand up and state what our topic is. She scoots lower in her chair and I take that as my cue to speak.

I stand up, hating how every single females' eyes in the room rake my body. "We're talking about human sex trafficking, specifically focusing on the trafficking of children."

"That is a very heavy topic, Mr. Hunter," the professor states, seemingly impressed.

"Yes, sir, very important, too," I reply.

"Okay, wonderful. So together this semester, we'll be trying to find solutions to problems like access to clean water, hunger relief, women's rights, child brides, clean energy, climate change, poverty, sexual education, and child sex trafficking, and one team will need to revisit their topic and get back to me by next class."

We continue to talk about the parts that make up a research

paper for the millionth time since I started college. We discuss every part of the paper from the introduction to the conclusion, and the professor gives us a piece of paper with the deadlines for each part. We review thesis statement formats, and well just about everything that has already been reviewed in our English classes before.

"Okay, now that we've run through that, let's talk about your homework."

Right on cue, heads hit desks and groans come to life. You'd think people would complain less. It's been years of the same and their complaints have changed nothing.

"Don't sound so excited. Remember in this class, you are heroes. Your homework is to find ten articles on your topic. These articles must come from primary or secondary sources. They must be peer-reviewed, and it goes without saying, but Wikipedia and Buzzfeed do not count. You have five minutes before class ends, so figure out how you want to tackle this assignment with your teammates."

The energy in the room rises along with the volume of chatter.

I turn to Mia. "So, how do you want to do this?"

"Well, we could meet tomorrow? I'm free if you are."

"I can't," I respond, and I see her turn her face away, hiding her red cheeks. "I have practice tomorrow," I add, feeling the need to explain myself.

"All day? Because I didn't tell you when I'd be free," she says smiling like a smartass who thinks she just caught me in a lie.

"I have class, and when I don't have class, I have practice. We have homecoming this weekend, which is also family weekend, so there's a lot of pressure." I don't understand why I continue to explain myself. If anyone else were asking, I would have walked away already.

"Oh," she states while nodding in understanding. "I guess I'll do the assignment then."

"Clift says he wants ten. Zack and I will do seven. You can do three. We'll work on it, and I'll text you when we finish so that we don't end up with the same ones."

"Okay, that works. Just…" She stops.

"Just, what?" I urge.

"Just don't forget to text me this time."

I'm about to remind her why I 'forgot' the last time when Abby wedges herself between us.

"Hey, handsome," she purrs, and I'm immediately consumed with rage. When will she finally get it?

"Abby," I say shortly "Can't you see I'm busy talking to—" I turn to where Mia is and her name dies on my lips. She's gone. Nowhere in sight. I look at the door, briefly catching a glimpse of her walking out.

"You're not busy anymore," Abbigail says smugly.

"Abby, I've told you a million times—"

"Yeah, I know," she says, cutting me off. "Don't worry. I don't want a relationship with you, but can we at least keep doing what we used to? You know I can be a lot of fun." She runs her hand up my arm as she leans in for a kiss. I back up, causing her to stumble.

"Not interested," I respond without hesitation. I don't want to keep doing what I used to. I want something else—someone else.

"Not possible," she counters.

"Fuck off, Abbigail." I know it's rude, but I've tried being nice. I've even tried being assertive, and she's still not getting it. I pick up my playbook, throw my bag over my shoulder and stalk out.

MIA

I've been trying not to think about what happened after class on

Monday. The blonde who'd inserted herself into our conversation and demanded all Colton's attention was the same girl from the party—the same girl he claims isn't his girlfriend.

"Someone should tell her that," I mutter to myself, letting out a sigh as I lounge on my bed. My phone pings and I grope around for it blindly. When I look at the screen, I see it's a text from Colton.

'Zack and I got the sources and I've emailed them to you.'

I respond faster than I should, overpowered by my excitement. I'd given up hope of him texting me altogether.

'I'm surprised that you remembered to text me [this time].'

Anxiously, I await his response, watching the icon that shows he's typing a reply. The dots start then stop. This happens again and again. Irritated, I drop the phone on the bed and start looking through my drawers for my most comfortable pajamas. I open the lowest drawer on my bureau and find my favorite pair of pants. Yes, they have Anna and Elsa's faces pasted on them, but what can I say? I really enjoyed the movie.

I glance at my phone, biting my lip. I hope he's taken my jab as a joke. I don't want to rub him the wrong way. Despite my initial impression of him, I've discovered I don't actually hate him. He's a good guy, he's a good group member and he has his shit together.

As I'm pulling on my pajamas my phone starts to ring.

It's an unknown number. I press the button, answering the call.

"Hello?" I say, using my rehearsed super professional voice—you never know who could be calling.

"I told you why I didn't text last time." Colton's voice comes over the line, a little rougher on the phone than in person. If it's possible, he sounds even sexier now.

"Because you're a hibernating bear. Also, why aren't you texting me now?" Not that I'm complaining. His voice is better than any text.

"I'm as big as a bear, but I don't know about the cuddly part. I told you; I slept because I was exhausted, and I called because I hate texting."

I move over to the bed, lying on my back and getting comfortable. I hope this conversation is a long one. "Hmm, I'm sure you're likely a closet cuddler. And yeah, no one is going to buy that excuse. You slept a whole day? Also, no texts means you're a grandpa," I say even though I personally hate texting too.

"I guess I could be into cuddling. Want to find out?" he says and my breathing hitches.

"I'd rather not."

"You sure about that?" he says his voice dropping down lower.

I imagine being wrapped in his arms and a sigh escapes my lips.

"So, why do you need to sleep a whole day?" I ask, evading the topic.

"I have classes, and then football practice, followed by mandatory gym sessions twice a day."

"These all sound like excuses to me."

"You would think differently if you had to do it yourself."

"Too bad I don't play football."

"Even then, I bet you wouldn't be able to keep up with my schedule for a day, let alone a week, without football."

"So, gym and class? What makes you think I don't already do that? Are you insinuating I'm unfit?"

"I'm saying your gym routine isn't as regimented as mine."

"I don't go, if you were wondering, but I'm sure I could keep up without needing a full day of sleep to recover. And without forgetting to text," I add, baiting him.

"Okay, I'll pick you up next Monday."

"For what?"

"For the gym. Have you been listening to this conversation at all, Collins? Am I boring you?"

"I never said I was going to the gym, and yeah, you're a little dry."

He chuckles. "So, you can't keep up. I guess I was right. That was easy, Collins. I thought you were better than that. And you're funny, you know I'm the highlight of your night."

"I can keep up, and I'm definitely not easy, Hunter."

"So, we'll start Monday then. You'll join me for at least a week."

"I have to spend a whole week with you?"

"Don't sound so bothered by the thought of spending time with me. Any other girl would jump at the chance."

Right, thanks for the reminder of the many girls in line waiting to get their claws in you.

"I'm not one of them," I reply a little too sharply. "Why would I even agree to this? What's in it for me?"

"From what I remember of your embarrassing loss at beer pong, you're quite competitive. The chance to redeem yourself should be motivation enough, but if it isn't, I'm happy to do whatever you want." His voice has become progressively huskier, and the sound of it tightens the muscles in the lower half of my body.

"Beating you is enough, but getting you to do what I want might come in handy. What's in it for you?" I ask, already coming up with all the things I could get him to do.

"The same. I'll get to redeem myself for not texting you, and you'll have to do anything I ask."

"I can agree to that, so long as nothing sexual is involved."

"I wouldn't need a bet for that," he says.

If he could see my face right now, I think I'd die. "You sure you want to do this?" I ask again, trying to ignore the cause of my racing heart.

"What's up, Collins? You worried?"

"No, you should be though. I'll have to start thinking about what I'll have you do when you lose."

"You haven't known me for long, but you should know I don't lose, especially when I have an incentive to win."

I can just imagine him smirking. "We'll see, grandpa."

"I'm sure you will, Mia."

There was a pause in the conversation, his breathing the only sign we were still on the phone.

"What are you up to?" he asks.

"Lying in bed. You?"

"Same."

"That's kind of lame. Aren't you supposed to be out partying, getting wasted and getting laid?"

"You think that little of me?" He sounds a little hurt.

"Just repeating what everyone else says."

"Do you always listen to what others say?"

"Not really."

"Good."

"Make sure you wear workout clothes. No heels necessary," Colton says to me.

It's Sunday night and we have been on the phone for roughly an hour, talking about everything and nothing at once. This is the second day in a row that we've talked on the phone, and it feels like we've been doing it for years. We have plans to go to the gym tomorrow, per our agreement. All morning, I've been thinking about what I got myself into with this stupid bet. I hate the gym, and I don't know how I'm supposed to resist Colton if I maximize my time with him.

"I've been to a gym before. It's not a foreign concept, you know."

"Booty shorts and a sports bra sound good to me."

"Yeah, in your dreams, Colton."

"Every night."

I feel my cheeks heat up.

I struggle to find a response and Colton speaks again. "So, I'll be picking you up at five."

I shoot up from my bed like it's lava and I'm burning. "Excuse me, you'll be what?"

"Yeah, you said you could keep up. Are you getting cold feet, Collins?"

"I can keep up, Hunter. But really? 5 a.m. is an ungodly hour. I can barely get up for our 8 a.m. class."

"It's what I do, babe. You've got to walk a week in my shoes. That was the deal."

I ignore the fact that he calls me babe because I refuse to go to a place where this is more than just flirting.

"Your shoes stink," is my response then add, "I'll be ready for five, but don't expect me to be happy about it. I won't be. I will not be chirpy; I am not one of those people."

"Wasn't expecting you to be. I didn't think you were the chirpy type."

"You annoy me," I respond as a giggle escapes my mouth.

A giggle, seriously?

"But you like me anyway."

He has no idea how true his words are. I know he doesn't really mean it in the way I take it, but I can't help acknowledging the feelings I have for him have surpassed hate, and friendship, and are moving to a less safe territory. They have been since the day I met him.

"I hate to break it to you, but I'm not one of your groupies," I tease.

"I know. Trust me, I know," he says, seeming almost content to acknowledge the difference.

"Anyway, I'll let you go. If I have to get up at the ass crack of dawn, I better hit the hay now."

"You'll be fine. I mean, seeing me first thing in the morning sounds like more than enough motivation to get you up."

"You think really highly of yourself, don't you?"

"Not high enough, I'd say."

"Hunter, you are swimming in an ocean of humbleness," I say sarcastically.

"Care to take a dip?"

I can imagine his eyebrows raising toward the sky suggestively. "Not a fan of swimming in oceans. Good night, Colton."

"We can change that. Good night, Mia." The way my name rolls off his tongue hits me straight in the stomach, resuscitating the butterflies I find myself trying to silence. It's almost like he's claiming me, and I find myself wanting nothing more than for it to be true. I want to be his. I want him to be mine and that scares the shit out of me.

"Hey, Mia?" Colton's voice breaks my thoughts.

"Yeah," I croak in response, unaware he'd been on the line. Thank God I hadn't said any of this out loud.

"Penny for your thoughts?"

"My thoughts are worth more than pennies, Colton. Go away."

"Okay, Okay. You hang up."

"Gladly," I say, ending the call. There's no way I'm playing the 'you hang up, no, you hang up' game. I'm already hanging, or at least my heart is.

Chapter Thirteen

MIA

"I hate you," I say as I hop into the passenger side of Colton's car. It's five in the morning. Who gets up this early?

"Good morning to you, too."

"Still hate you."

"Yeah, yeah. Of course you do. Here." He hands me a cup of coffee and I grab it from him like I've been denied caffeine for a year. I sniff it, feeling myself coming alive.

"I guess you love me now. It's a pleasure to deal you drugs," he says, shifting into first.

"Please stop. I'm not ready for you yet." I take a sip of the coffee only to realize it's just the way I like it: no milk, enough sugar.

"I'll keep it down until we get to the gym then," he says with a laugh.

"The coffee hasn't kicked in, but thanks for getting it just how I like it." I can't believe he remembered how I'd ordered it at the diner.

"Wouldn't think of getting you anything else."

"You're quite perceptive," I say, voicing the thought running through my mind.

"I have to be. On that note, I've gotta say I'm kind of disappointed you decided to skip the shorts and sports bra."

"I'm still wearing a sports bra, Colton. Not that it's any of your business, but I keep it under my shirt. Now drive before I go back inside and drop into bed."

"Is that an invitation to join you?" he asks.

"You wish."

"You keep saying that. Maybe you're the one that's wishing it."

"Nope, never. No thanks."

"You are just a peach in the mornings. We should do this more often," he says. I stare at him ferally. "Okay, okay. I'm driving, Miss Daisy."

Ha ha, very funny.

A few minutes later, we arrive at the athletic center. I'm a little shocked it's not the general gym near the quad; this one is situated near the football field, and is typically reserved for athletes. The rest of us 'normal' people go to the Murray Center.

I turn to Colton. "I don't think I'm allowed in there," I tell him, pointing at the facility. Honestly, I'm not disappointed that we won't be working out at the butt-crack of dawn.

His eyebrows bunch in confusion. "Why wouldn't you be?"

"Kiya told me this gym is for athletes only."

"You're fine."

"You don't recognize rules, do you? If you do, you're probably the type that doesn't follow them either, huh?"

"Football players get some perks," he responds nonchalantly.

I roll my eyes. "Of course football players get perks."

"Mia, stop trying to find excuses to bail and let's go." He smiles. "Unless you're ready to call it quits?"

There's no way I'm giving him the satisfaction of winning. "Not a quitter. Let's go."

We walk into the gym side by side, and I can see that we're not the only ones here. I guess athletes do have to put some work in. I spot the locker room, and move in that direction with Colton on my tail. We both go to our respective locker rooms, where I drop off my bag, grab my water bottle, phone, and headphones, and head out. I wait for Colton to exit the locker room too, and when he does, I find myself rediscovering his body. Long gone is the long-sleeved sweatshirt and sweatpants. In their place are a workout t-shirt—the Under Armour kind that hugs his muscles perfectly—and basketball shorts, which do little to hide his assets. He really knows how to make my mission impossible.

He bumps my shoulder, ending my reverie. "You ready?"

"As I'll ever be," I state.

"If you want, you can quit now."

"And give you the satisfaction? No thanks."

"Okay, well, do you want me to go easy on you?"

"I'm sure I can keep up, Hunter."

"You sure? Last chance to bail."

"If I weren't sure I could take you, I wouldn't be here."

"When you say it that way," he says, and I realize how that may have sounded.

"Anyway," I say, ignoring his suggestive comment. "Let's start."

Colton makes his way to the left of the treadmills, where a bunch of mats have been thrown on the floor.

"Okay, first we're going to stretch so you don't pull a muscle and need me to carry you out."

I roll my eyes at that but I join him on the mat and begin stretching. "Just so you know, I'd be out of here already if I didn't love to win."

"I'm not too sure about that," he says.

"Of course you aren't. So, what's the plan for today?"

"As soon as we finish stretching, we'll do two miles on the treadmill to get our heart rates going." If only he knew my heart is already working in overdrive.

"Then?" I ask.

"Then, we'll do push-ups, crunches, sit-ups, and some mild lifting," he says with a cocky smirk, waiting for me to give up.

"Sounds easy enough."

"You say that now."

"I'll say it later, too."

He grins. "Okay, today we'll do five sets of ten push-ups."

"Is that what you normally do?" I ask, making sure he isn't taking it easy on me, but hoping that he doesn't do like two hundred of them. My will can only take me so far; my physical strength will definitely be an obstacle.

"Just fifty today since we'll be lifting later. We don't want to overwork the arms."

"Okay, ready when you are," I say, avoiding his eyes as I finish stretching.

He stands up and extends his hand to me. I wrap my fingers around his, and he pauses for a few seconds before lifting me up to a standing position. He walks to the treadmills, and I follow behind, still admiring his body. I hop on the treadmill, pull out my cell phone, plug in the headphones and scroll through my playlists until I find my workout list—my seldom used workout playlist.

"You going to ignore me?" Colton asks.

"Do you normally talk when you run?"

"No."

"That's what I thought."

He smiles this picture-perfect smile and shakes his head, pulling out his headphones and phone. I press play on my playlist, place the device into the cup holder, and touch the 'quick start' button on the machine. I start running to the sound of "Wake Up" by Kesha, hoping it gives me some energy. If I'm going to keep up with Colton, I'm going to need it.

Out of the corner of my eye, I catch a glimpse of him running effortlessly beside me. I pick up speed to match him because at this pace he'll be done way before me. I'm only supposed to keep up, but keeping up means following the pace he sets.

About thirteen minutes later, I see Colton get off the treadmill. The asshole can run. I still have half a mile to go. I watch him grab some paper towels and spray to clean down his machine. When he's done, he comes to stand behind me, and the hair on the back of my neck prickles at the knowledge he's watching me. I finish three minutes later and wipe down the machine.

"Not bad, Collins."

"Next thing," I command, breathlessly.

"Push-ups," he says, returning to the place where we started stretching. "Okay, so I'll demonstrate how to do a proper push-up."

"I know how to do—"

"Not the kind they have girls doing in gym class," he clarifies.

"I know how to do a push-up, Colton."

"Well just in case, we'll alternate sets. I'll go first." Before I have a chance to suggest we both do it at the same time, he lowers himself to the ground and starts. I swear it takes him only two minutes to lift his body up and down ten times. He moves so effortlessly, like he's lifting a feather and not his two-hundred-pound body.

"Your turn," he says, tagging me on the shoulder. I lower myself to the ground and start.

Up. Down. Up. Down.

It felt like Colton did his set in seconds. Mine feel like they're taking me hours.

"You," I state, feeling like it's the matchup of a lifetime, both of us seeing how far we can push the other. I take advantage of my rest and watch as Colton's muscular arms work. I'd told myself I was going to make every effort to ignore him. But my efforts are futile. I am acutely aware of his every move.

Push-ups, crunches, and sit-ups. None of these things have ever been sexier, but watching Colton do his sets makes them the most entertaining things in the world.

"Want to quit now?" he asks after we finish the five sets of push-ups, crunches, and sit-ups. My body screams yes! telling me to stop this madness, but my stubborn head says no. There's only lifting left. I can do this.

"No. Stop asking. Let's finish this," I state, my breaths coming out in short, sharp bursts, making it clear that I never do this shit.

"Okay, so we'll do some lifting. You'll spot me so I can show you the proper way of lifting, then I'll spot you."

"You're adamant to show me things today."

"I'd like to show you things every day," he says, and I can't help but smile at his comment.

"Isn't spotting someone a very important task?"

"Yes, so?"

"So, you might need someone *mas fuerte*."

"I lost you after 'someone'."

"Sorry. Someone stronger," I say, hating the fact that I have to admit weakness. I'd rather that than drop the weights on him.

"Was that Spanish? And are you saying you're not strong enough?"

"Yes, and I'm saying I don't know how much you lift."

"Where are you from?" he asks, adjusting the weight on the bar.

"Dominican Republic. I told you that when we talked about climbing trees," I deadpan.

"No, I mean where did you live before coming here?" he asks, rephrasing his question.

"California. Are you really going to have me spot you?" I ask, changing the topic. He's lying on the bench now, sweat glistening on his skin.

"Yeah, it's not hard. I don't ever have someone spot me. I know my limits," he says, his eyes holding mine.

"If you say so," I say, not feeling at all confident.

"I do say so." He winks and starts to lift the weights. "Your job is really to make sure the bar doesn't fall on my face. I'll tell you if I need help setting it back in place."

"Doesn't sound at all important," I mutter, taking my position like I've seen it done on TV.

I watch the way his muscles expand every time he lifts the bar, and for a second I wish…nothing.

"Yes?" I ask with an unsteady voice when I notice he's looking at me.

"Nothing," he says, equally out of breath. I take note of the sweat on his forehead, the way his chest moves up and down, the tight fit of his shirt. And well, I've never found someone covered in sweat sexy before, but there's a first time for everything.

Colton sets the bar back in place.

"Done already?" I ask having lost count of how many reps he's done.

"Nope, just taking a break."

"I thought someone like you would have stamina."

"I can show you better than I can tell you."

I laugh at his likely unintentional quoting of *Bring It On: All or Nothing*.

Colton resumes his workout. God, the sounds coming from him are mesmerizing. I never thought the sound of someone working out would be so attractive, but on Colton, I don't know what wouldn't be. I can feel each grunt in places I shouldn't, and my mind starts to wonder where else he might make these sounds.

"Done. Your turn."

"Okay, just so I know, this is the last thing I need to do, right?"

"Yeah, we'll switch it up throughout the week."

"Can we just call it even after today?"

"Can't handle it?"

"Don't want to wake up at five o'clock every day."

"We'll see how you do and I might consider it."

"You're annoying."

"I'm a lot of things. How many pounds do you want to lift?"

"Can't I do the same amount as you?"

"I don't think you'd want to."

"How many did you do?"

"Three hundred, but I do this every day. And while you do a decent job of faking it, I can tell you couldn't lift that much."

"Give me seventy-five. I'll start with that."

"Wow, you acquiesced faster than I thought you would."

"I know my limits," I respond quoting him. I take his place on the bench while he gets up and stands above me. He doesn't say anything else, he just breathes and watches me. My skin prickles and goosebumps break out, betraying me. I don't know which I'd rather have: his eyes off me or on because both elicit a reaction.

"Well, well, well," a voice says from behind me. I keep lifting, the seventy-five pounds feeling heavier with every rep.

"'Sup," I hear Colton reply.

"If I knew you were training people, I would have signed up long ago, Colt."

"Right? I would have put my name on the list." I hear Zack's distinct voice.

"Who's the chick?" the other voice asks again, and I stop my workout, letting Colton help me set the bar back in its place.

"Don't you have something better to do, Jesse?" Colton replies, and I sit up.

"Why, hello there," Zack says to me.

"Hey, Zack," I respond, a little out of breath. My eyes move to see another guy standing to one side. I don't recognize him, but his blond hair and distinct jaw are familiar.

"Fancy seeing you here."

Zack's comment drags my attention back to him. "Fancy seeing you at all," I say, reminding him of how many times he's missed class already.

"I gotta do what I gotta do."

"Hopefully that means going to class today?" I reply.

"So, you all know each other," the other guy says. He's tall, dark-haired and broad-shouldered. This must be Jesse. "I don't think the two of us have been formally introduced. You must be Colton's g—" He stops, looking at Colton.

"Mia. She's Mia," Colton finishes for him.

"Hi, Mia. I'm Jesse Falcon, kicker, pre-med, and confidante to these assholes," he says, extending his hand toward me.

"Hi, Jesse. I'm just Mia."

"I don't know about that if you've got this guy training you." He jabs a thumb in Colton's direction.

"Not training me," I clarify. "Just a bet."

"A bet?" Zack says from his spot next to Colton.

"Tell me more," Jesse says.

"What's going on?" the mysterious blond says, joining the conversation.

"Your brother here is giving private lessons because of some sort of bet," Jesse says.

Brother? I look at the guy more closely and I can see the similarities to Colton; they're striking. The differences are few, but they're there. While Colton looks like a man, his brother looks more fratty—boyish. Colton is taller and more muscular, but his brother is well on his way too. Still, Colton is far more handsome and looks like he could take his brother any day.

"Fuck." I hear the word escape Colton's lips and I can tell he's annoyed his friends are here. He rubs his sweaty forehead as we both stand there. Surrounded by these giants, I'm reminded of how short I am.

"Nice to meet you, Mia. I'm Nick," he says with a shit-eating grin on his face.

"Hello," I say a little guarded and see Colton shake his head.

"I've heard a lot about you. It's good to finally put a face to the name," he says and I'm a little scared of what he may have heard.

"No, he hasn't," Colton states through clenched teeth.

"Yeah, I have," Nick says, defying his brother. "Someone can't stop talking about you," he adds.

"Yeah, I keep telling all the guys about your fall on the second day of class, sorry," Zack adds with a shrug, and I laugh, feeling both embarrassed and relieved.

"Yup, always talking about the short pretty girl from his class who joined his group," Jesse adds.

"Um, thanks," I respond because what else can I say?

"Yeah, I would have called dibs, but—"

"But she's not property," Colton fires back.

"Not *my* property, that's for sure," Zack adds.

"Okay!" Colton announces. "Thank you so much for crashing our session. Mia and I were just finishing up."

"Really, bro? Can't stay for a few more minutes?" Nick asks, looking disappointed that he can't keep teasing his brother.

"Nope, all done," Colton adds, cleaning the bench I was just using.

"What's going on here?" says yet another guy. He's about the same height as Colton, and just as handsome as the others. It's like this school is full of GQ models.

"Colton is training Mia," Zack states.

"Apparently for some sort of bet," Jesse adds.

"What is the bet?" Nick asks, his interest piqued.

"None of your business," Colton replies and it's like watching a tennis match with all the back and forth. I'm getting a neck workout with how much they volley.

"I don't think we've met yet. I'm Chase, Colton's best friend."

"Nice to meet you too."

For first impressions, this one sucks. I'm sweaty and my hair is likely a mess.

"We were just leaving," Colton says, his words clipped.

"Nah, stay a little longer. We're not done talking to Mia yet, right, babe?" Nick says and Colton shoots daggers at him.

"Not *your* babe," Colton growls.

"Well boys, the show's over. Let's get to work," Chase says, noticing Colton's agitation level rising.

"But—"

Chase stops Nick by saying, "No buts. I'm the captain of the defensive line. I can make them do things to you that you can't even imagine."

"You ready?" Colton asks me as the guys go back and forth with Chase, forgetting we're here.

"Yup, all good," I reply, hoping he isn't ashamed of being seen with me.

"So, I've thought about what you said," he says as we walk towards the locker room, nodding at a few other people who've arrived.

"What did I say?" I've said many things today.

"That you didn't really want to wake up and do this every day."

"Okay! And?"

"I'll agree to that."

"What's the catch?"

"What makes you think there is one?"

"Well, is there?"

"Yes," he says with a smirk, the mood becoming light and flirty again.

"See?" I respond with a low chuckle.

"It's not bad."

"Okay, so if I agree to whatever you ask then it'll be like I won the bet?" I ask, hopeful.

"We'll call it even," he says as we reach the locker rooms.

COLTON

"Nope, I don't think so. I need to be able to tell people I won," she says with a glint of fire in her eyes, her competitiveness making her even more attractive. I'm glad Chase ran interference because I was seconds away from punching one of them for making her uncomfortable with all their questions.

"Okay, fine. So, I'll let you say you won if you agree to my terms."

She narrows her eyes at me. "What are your terms?"

"We don't do this every day," I say, signaling to the gym around us. "Instead," I pause for dramatic effect, because why the hell not?

"Instead?" she says urging me on.

"Instead, you meet me for coffee at the student café every day we have class together," I say, putting it all out there, hoping she accepts my proposal because I have the urge to spend more time with her.

This wasn't enough. I need more.

"For how long?" she asks.

"Until the end of the semester." *Or forever,* I add in my head for fear of sounding like a creep if I say it out loud.

"Sounds doable."

I give myself a mental high five. "Good."

"Just so you know, I won."

"Yes, yes, you did," I say with a secret smile. And so did I because she just gave me the in I needed.

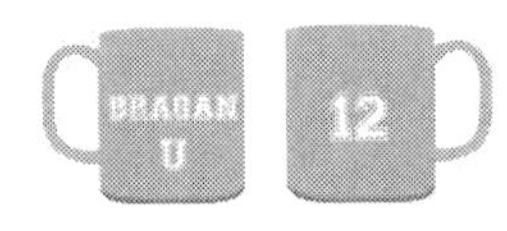

Chapter Fourteen

MIA

What the hell is that annoying sound?

I look at my alarm clock and see it's 5:58. Like, 5:58 in the morning. I'm supposed to have two more blissful minutes of sleep before my alarm rings. The noise continues, and I realize it's not my alarm—it's my phone.

I get up slowly, already knowing I'm going to be sore everywhere. Even lifting myself up from the bed is a task. I slowly move one leg and place it on the floor, the other following after. Goodness, I really should not have pushed myself so hard at the gym. If I thought how I felt yesterday was bad, this is hell. I slowly reach for my phone, my arms feeling like they're going to fall off.

Without bothering to look at the caller ID, I swipe right and answer.

"Hello?"

"Hey," the voice on the other line says at the same time my alarm clock starts ringing. Out of habit, I hit the snooze button.

"Colton?"

"Mia," he responds, and I can tell he's smiling.

"Are you okay?" I ask because something must be really wrong if he's calling me this early.

"Yes, I am."

I rub my eyes and a yawn escapes me. "Okay, so why are you calling me?"

"Am I not allowed to call you?"

"Not at five in the morning!"

"It's six."

"Same thing."

"Not really."

Not wanting to get dragged into the argument, I ask, "Why arc you calling?"

"Couldn't I have just wanted to talk to you? Do I need a reason?"

"Yes, yes you do. You need a reason to rob me of two minutes of precious sleep."

"Remember, I gave you the extra hour by allowing you to bail on our bet."

"I didn't bail. We made a deal."

"Yes, we did, and that's what I'm calling about."

"Really, at this time?"

"I just finished my workout."

"Thank you for thinking of me," I respond sarcastically.

"And we have a coffee date today." Date? Did he just say date?

"Are we already starting this new arrangement?" What does he have to gain by having coffee with me every day?

"Yes, that was the deal, unless you want to back out from that one too."

"No, you should already know I don't quit. But were you thinking about having coffee at 6 a.m.?"

"Not now," he says with a chuckle. "I just wanted to give you a heads up. What time do you leave your place to head to the coffee shop?"

"How do you know I head to a coffee shop after I leave my house?"

"Because I know you. I know you get coffee every day before class. I know you don't make it yourself because it would mean getting up earlier. So, the logical choice is the school café."

"How do you know I go to the school café?"

"Because it's on the way from your house to class, and I know you like to get to class early."

"You are starting to sound like a stalker, Colton."

"Not a stalker."

"No? Then what would you call yourself? You know how I like my coffee, you know I leave my house early every day to get some. What else do you know?"

"I know you like to get to class early because you like to mark your territory."

"And you say you're no stalker?" I mutter. I can't believe he knows so much about me in so little time.

"I'm just observant."

"Do you know this much information about everyone?"

"No, just those I pay attention to."

"Why are you paying attention to me?" I ask, still not believing this is the conversation I'm having at six in the freaking morning.

"Don't worry about it."

"Seriously?" Don't worry about it? That has got to be my most hated phrase.

"So, what time do you leave your house?"

"Twenty past seven."

"Okay, I'll be there."

I ask, "At the cafe? Hello? Colton?" But he's already hung up.

Stalling no longer, I plug my phone back in and get up from bed. I grab my towel and head over to the bathroom to start my morning routine. I brush my teeth, take a shower, and apply a little makeup—not because I'm going to see Colton, but just because it feels like a makeup kind of day. Then, I comb my hair and lift it into a sort of neat bun. I pick out a pair of light-blue jeans, ankle boots and a light pink sweater. I also grab a coat and a scarf, then switch out the books in my bag.

By the time I'm done, it's ten past seven. And since I'd rather be early than late, I decide to leave the house earlier than I'd told Colton I would. En route to the door, I pull my phone from the charger, toss my book bag over my shoulder, and look around the room once more to make sure there's nothing I'm missing.

As I step out the door, I'm stunned to find the most handsome man I've ever met waiting in my driveway. He's leaning on the front of his car, his eyes roaming my body hungrily.

COLTON

I'm done for. My brain is in overdrive as I see Mia. She takes me in from head to toe, and I do the same. She's beautiful, and I find myself way too attracted to her. So much so that I couldn't wait the extra fifteen minutes to meet her at the school café. Instead, I came over to her place because it would give us a few more minutes together before we go to class and sit next to each other for a couple of hours.

Isn't that stupid? Aren't I whipped? I'm whipped for sure, because here I stand in the cold just waiting for her to come out. For my girl to come outside and meet me. She may not know it yet, but I do—she's mine. And after yesterday, the guys know it too.

"What are you doing here?"

"Good morning to you, too," I respond with a big-ass smile because I can't help it. Just being around her brightens my mood.

"Not a good morning. I didn't get much sleep."

"Too busy thinking of me?" I ask jokingly, though I wish she had been thinking of me because I was thinking about her. I don't think I've stopped thinking about her since the first—well second—time I saw her.

"Too busy being woken up by you."

"I pegged you for an early riser; although, after yesterday I should have known better. Still, I didn't mean to wake you, though it was only two minutes. I figured you'd be up to get ready for class. Don't girls take hours to get ready?" I ask, making a generalization I know will bring fire to her eyes.

"No, it doesn't take me hours to get ready," she snaps irritably. "Could you stop painting all girls with one brush?"

When I only smile at her triumphantly, knowing I've pushed her buttons, she asks, "What are you doing here?"

"I'm picking you up for our date," I respond, emphasizing the word date. I'm giving her all the signs other girls would have jumped on weeks ago, but not Mia.

"I thought I was meeting you at the café," she says.

"I thought it would be best to pick you up."

She pulls at her sweater nervously. "Why is that?"

"Because it's cold outside." And I didn't want my girl to freeze. I break our staring contest as I move to the passenger side of the car and open the door for her.

"I'm okay with the cold. I can walk. I do it every day," she says, getting in.

"You won't need to because I'll be here to pick you up."

"Why would you do that?"

"Because we'll be going to the café together anyway, so if I pick you up, you can get more sleep and be less cold."

"Like I said, I'm okay. Plus, the days when we don't have coffee together, I'll have to walk anyway. It doesn't make a lot of a difference," she retorts because she can never just agree. She never makes it easy, and I think that's part of what attracts me to her.

"Easy solution. We'll have coffee every day, and I'll be picking you up," I reply, closing her door and walking over to the driver's side with a cocky ass grin because whether she realizes it or not, I'm making her mine.

Chapter Fifteen

COLTON

I've seen Mia every day for coffee since our one and only gym session. Today, I've asked her to meet me for lunch too. We're only eating at school, but I'll take whatever time I can get with her. I glance at the clock hanging on the wall above the professor's head and watch the minute hand edge closer to the hour. When we're finally dismissed, I pack up my things and am first out the door, but I'm drawn to a stop just outside the room when my phone rings.

It's Adaline. I don't call her anything but her first name. There are more fitting names out there for her, but out of self-respect, I refrain from using them. This woman only birthed me—nothing more. That's the only thing tying me to her, that and…

"What do you want?" I ask, clutching my phone so hard it creaks.

"Hello to you too, son," she replies in her false motherly tone.

"Do you need something?" I ask, walking toward the dining hall.

"Yes, as a matter of fact, I do. The ladies and I are throwing an event to raise money for at-risk youth," she says like she actually cares about the problem. If she did, she'd be there for Nick and

Kaitlyn, who regularly put themselves in danger just to get her attention.

"Good for you," I respond sarcastically, hoping to end the conversation as quickly as possible.

"You're coming. It's this Sunday at six. Your brother will be there too as you're both young men in college, and we want you to talk to some of the youth."

"Can't. I'm busy."

"Clear your schedule," she bites out.

"I have homework."

"You don't need brains, sweetheart. Your talent will get you into the NFL. This is important."

I can feel my anger rising. "I'm not going."

"I'm not asking," she says before hanging up the phone.

When I walk into the dining hall, my anger is still riding me hard. I like having control, yet I can't control my own damn life with Adaline pulling my strings like I'm her fucking puppet. I scan the room for Mia, finding her at a table with all the guys. They're laughing at something she's saying, her hands moving animatedly as she retells a joke or a story.

As I approach, she looks up and seems to instantly sense my bad mood. I sit down beside her, and I can see her staring at me from the corner of my eye. I try to give her a reassuring smile, but I know it doesn't reach my eyes. My thoughts are too consumed with Adaline and her ridiculous demands. I am not at her beck and call.

I try to push away my anger and instead focus on Mia and the guys. They're giving her shit because she hasn't gone to a football game yet. She tells them about her love of professional football, and agrees to maybe watch a game at some point. I pick at my lunch and try to keep up with the rest of the conversation, but my mind is elsewhere. I sense Mia look at me over her shoulder a few times, and I can see the worry written on her face.

I glance at my phone, checking the time. "Shit." I look at Mia. "I've got to go."

"It's fine," she replies, looking down at her tray.

"Can I see you later?"

Her brows rise. "Three times in one day?"

If only she knew I'd happily see her every second of the day. "Are you free? We need to figure out how to tackle the assignment."

She smiles tentatively. "Sure."

"Great. I'll pick you up at eight."

After practice finishes, I rush home to shower then go and pick up Mia for our library date. I turn on my car, getting ready to shift it into gear, when my phone starts to ring. The last time I checked my phone, I had three voicemails, five text messages, and four missed calls from Adaline. A quick look down at the screen tells me it's her again. I ignore the call, but Adaline can be persistent when she wants to, so two missed calls later, she's still calling. With a growl, I answer the phone, mentally preparing myself for another shitty conversation.

"Did you cancel your plans?" she asks in lieu of a greeting.

Good. It's better this way. At least the conversation will be shorter. "No. I told you I have homework to do," I lie again.

"You'll be there at six tomorrow, Colton."

"Did you hear me?" I ask. "I said no, I can't make it."

"It's sweet that you think you have a choice. You'll be there at six, and you know the consequences if you don't show."

"I'm not showing," I respond, calling her bluff. No way she'll follow through with her threats just because I don't show up to a staged meet and greet with some kids.

"You will do whatever I—"

I cut the call before she can finish. Maybe this is risky, but there's only so much I can take.

I drive faster than usual over to Mia's place. Once again, I'm not in the greatest mood, but I know that seeing her will make it better, even if it's only temporarily. The moment I pull into her driveway, she comes running out the door with one of those jackets with the furry hoods and goes straight to the passenger side like she has every day since the gym.

She looks like she belongs in this car with me, and for a second, I can feel my mood begin to lighten.

Then my phone rings again.

"You going to pick that up?" Mia asks after a long minute of listening to Adaline's assigned ringtone.

"No," I respond tightly.

I know she's calling to threaten me again. To get me to bend to her demands like she always does. I know if I pick it up, I'll cave because there's too much at stake.

"Are you okay?" she asks.

"Yeah," I lie. "Why wouldn't I be?"

MIA

"I'm not in the mood for this," Colton snaps, slamming his hands on the top of the table. A few people turn our way, but the moment they see Colton, they abandon any thoughts of telling him to shut up.

"Oh," I respond, not knowing what else to say, but feeling like I've crossed an invisible line. "My bad." I start gathering up my things that are scattered all over the table. I am *not* about to stand here and get my ass chewed for suggesting we interview his parents for this assignment instead of mine—the parents I don't have.

"No, Mia, wait. I'm sorry. I'm being an asshole."

"You don't say. Don't expect me to disagree." Maybe I should have stuck to my gut feeling about him. First impressions and all. I jam my notebook into my bag.

"I don't."

"Colton, your mood has more swings than a playground and I'm no longer a child." I zip up my bag, throwing it over my shoulder.

"Fuck," he says, pulling at his hair. I grab my coat from the back of the chair and start to put it on.

"We can't interview my parents."

"Why not?" I question while zipping my jacket up.

"Why can't we just interview yours?" he says, sounding defeated.

"Because I don't have any," I say in a really low voice. I need to walk away before I say something I regret.

The breeze hits me the moment I open the door, the winter air chilling my bones. Thank God, I listened to Kiya and put this coat on. My first New England winter would have been brutal without one. Still, as I walk under the stars, I know the move here was a good choice. I adjust the hood trying my best to shield against the wind.

I walk in the direction of my apartment, trying to erase from my mind the exchange with Colton. I'm so sick of his changing attitude—first the gym after his friends joined us, then the cafeteria, and now. He can be flirty, funny, and cute one minute, and then lethal the next.

"Mia, wait up!" I hear him say from behind me, but I keep walking. I'm *not* wasting my time. "Can you stop walking so fast. I'm trying to talk to you."

I don't slow down. "I was trying to talk to you, too. Remember?" He comes up on my right, matching my every stride.

"I'm sorry about your parents," he says and he sounds sincere.

"Me too," I respond, because what else am I supposed to say, 'it's okay'? Because it's not. "I'm sorry you're an asshole," I add.

"Me, too," he says and we both burst out laughing, the earlier tension being blown away by the breeze.

"What happened to them?"

"I think you might have multiple personalities."

"Most people just see the asshole. You're one of the lucky ones that get to see all of them."

"Lucky me," I say sarcastically.

After a beat, he asks, "So, your parents?"

I give him a sideways glance. He seems adamant in learning more. I turn to face him. "I'll tell you about mine if you tell me about yours."

His jaw hardens immediately, the light gray in his eyes turning to a dark metal, and I see his demeanor change, shutting me out like I've seen him do to his friends.

In that split-second, I decide to stop the barrier from separating Colton from me. I can tell whatever he's hiding has been affecting him. The person he just became before me is the same one I bumped into that night at the club. The guy that walks around like he doesn't have any emotions, and doesn't give a fuck about anything. But I can tell there's more to it. There's more to him.

Don't judge a book by its cover, right? This cover doesn't seem as inviting but I'm already invested in the story.

I know how difficult it is to talk about your feelings. If anyone knows, it's the girl that switched schools and moved across the country to avoid talking about hers. So here I am, laying it all out for him. Giving him yet another piece of me.

"You don't have to—tell me that is. I can tell you about mine, and if you want to, if you feel comfortable, if you trust me, you can talk to me."

I look him in the eyes, my right hand finding its way to his jaw, my eyes connecting with his. I want him to feel the sincerity of my words. His eyes go back to that beautiful gray that makes my heart flutter. He sighs, his body relaxing, and I can see the wall disappear.

"I'm sorry for acting like a jerk," he says. "I'd love to know more about you. I promise I'm not always a dick."

I notice my left hand is on his chest, while my right is still caressing his face. I pull away immediately.

"I'm sure you'll do it again, but don't expect me to stand here and take it."

"I wouldn't dream of it. I'll work on it," he murmurs.

"Shouldn't you be heading in the direction of your car?" I ask, remembering that we drove here.

"I'll get it later. Unless you'd rather I drive you hom—"

"I'd like to walk," I answer feeling like it'll help take away some of the awkwardness between us.

We walk to my house in silence, enjoying each other's company. As soon as we hit the front door, I turn to say goodnight, but he blind-sides me by saying, "Can I come in? I'd like to hear about your parents." His voice is tender, his usual confidence gone. As much as it petrifies me to share this with him, a part of me knows that I have to, that I want to.

I nod, open the door, and he follows me inside.

"What do you think?" I open my arms, and do a weird motion to display my apartment which I immediately regret.

"This place is amazing! Is that a piano?" Colton says as he walks into the living room.

"Nope, that is a bicycle," I respond catching up to him.

"Sarcasm suits you, Collins. You play?" He presses a few keys offbeat.

"I love board games."

"The piano, woman! Do you play the piano?" he asks as he sits on the bench.

"Yeah, sometimes," I respond while watching him look like he belongs here.

"Could you play for me?" He asks with hopeful eyes. There's no semblance of the Colton from the library.

"One thing at a time, young one."

"You are weird," he says, getting up and walking around.

"I know, thanks."

"Should I be afraid?"

"Yes. Be very afraid," I say jokingly. But really the one that should be afraid is me. Afraid that I'm letting him in only to be hurt by him.

"Got it," he says, nodding. A smile appears on his face, and oh what it does to me.

"Want anything to drink?"

"Do you have any beer?"

"We only have tequila and rum." Courtesy of Kiya.

"Seriously, you have tequila but no beer?"

I shrug my shoulders. "Kiya likes tequila, I like rum. It's just how we do."

"It's how you end up with an insane hangover."

"You would know." I wink and he laughs.

"It's also how you end up sleeping in another person's bed."

"Yeah, luckily for me the guy wasn't a complete douche and decided to sleep in a different room."

"Said who?"

"Said Kiya. Thank you for that, by the way. But also, you suck for making me freak out. I legit thought I had slept in the same room as you."

"Jeez, Mia. You don't have to say it like it would be repugnant for us to share the same air."

"We're sharing the same air right now, and trust me it's not that great," I tease, grabbing two bottles of water from the fridge and handing him one.

"You let me in. You can't mind my presence too much." He opens his water, taking a sip. "Where's Kiya?" he asks changing the subject.

"She has class till late, then study group, I think."

"We're on our own?"

"Yes," I respond while taking a seat on the couch. Colton joins me, taking the seat next to me.

"Are you ready to listen?" I ask, wanting to get it over with. I don't want to prolong the inevitable.

"I'm always ready to listen to anything you've got to say."

I take a deep breath and begin recounting the story. "Well, my mom died in a car accident about a year ago."

"I'm so sor—"

"And before you say you're sorry, let me warn you, I don't want your pity. I've dealt with it. I've moved on. Apologies are not necessary. You didn't hurt me."

Not yet anyway, the voice inside my head chimes in.

"Okay, I'm so—" He catches himself mid-apology. "I understand."

I tell him all about how my father became addicted to gambling, then turned to alcohol. I tell him how my parents began to fight every night and how my mother got struck by a driver that had run a red light at an intersection while she was on her way to pick up my drunk father from his favorite bar. Colton doesn't say anything. He just nods and listens, and I appreciate him for it. The fact that I can talk about it with such ease is a sign that I'm actually moving on, or at least I think that's what a psychologist would say.

"My dad couldn't take the guilt, I guess, so after losing mom, he left."

Colton's hand lands on my shoulder—not in a sexual way, but in a comforting and supporting one. It's like he really understands and wants to give me strength. I finish my story, ready to never relive it again. Although I'm moving forward, the memories still hold a lot of pain.

"Thank you for sharing that with me," he says after I've finished.

"Now you know why we can't interview my parents."

"We can't interview mine either. I have my reasons, and I'll share them with you, but only when I'm ready."

"Okay. Take all the time you need. I'll be here."

"Thank you," he says.

And I know he means it. This right here, this is what I was afraid of. We're both comfortable with each other, trusting each other, and it feels like we're moving past just being friends. It's not getting close to him that I'm afraid of. It's what happens after.

"Okay, story time over. Do you want to watch a movie?" I ask. I don't want the night to end. I'm not ready for him to leave.

"Sure. Your pick though," he says, kicking off his shoes and laying his head on my lap. Although this proximity and level of comfort should make me run for the hills, it doesn't – it feels… right. I grab the remote from the table, search through the movies we've purchased and find one of the Fast and Furious movies. There really is nothing like Paul Walker, Vin Diesel, cars, and speed to end a rollercoaster of a night.

"You're perfect," I think I hear him say.

"What?" I ask.

"Perfect, I said. Great movie choice."

MIA

I'm startled awake when a bright light hits my eyes.

"Well, well, well."

Confusion kicks in when I see Kiya staring down at me with a big ass smile on her face.

I try to sit up, but the weight of Colton's arm around my stomach stops me.

How did we even end up in this position?

"What's so funny?"

"Oh, you know, walking in to find you cuddling on the couch with the hottest guy on campus."

"Keep it down," I hiss, glancing over my shoulder to check he hasn't woken up. "We fell asleep watching a movie." I point to the TV, which is off.

Traitor.

"Yup, that's it. Lucky for me, I got a picture," she teases.

"Kiya! You know we didn't do anything else. You need to erase that photo. Now."

"Anyway, I'm exhausted and I don't want to interrupt the lovers."

"We're not lovers! Erase the photo, Kiya!" I look out the window, seeing the streetlights are still on outside. "What time is it?" I ask.

"It's 2 a.m."

"What the heck were you doing out so late?"

"Not watching a movie with Blake."

"Gross!" I finally manage to free myself from Colton and get up from the couch. "When did you decide to give him a chance?"

"When he asked me to be his girl," she answers casually, like it's no big deal. Kiya points at Colton's massive body. "What are you going to do about him?"

I run my eyes over him. He's so large he doesn't fit on the couch. I don't even know how the two of us managed to sleep there.

"Just let him sleep. He's got to be at the gym in about three hours, and you and I will have a talk about Blake in the morning," I say, giving her my best 'I mean business look'.

She gives me a sly grin. "You know an awful lot about his schedule."

"We have class together. We're also working on a project together."

"That's all? He seems to be investing an awful lot of time into this project. It must be very important."

"That's all. Trust me."

Kiya's teasing expression disappears. "Is that all you want it to be?"

I look back at Colton's sleeping figure. "It doesn't matter."

"It might."

"It won't." I grab one of the blankets we keep under the coffee table and cover Colton. Kiya, seeing that the conversation isn't going anywhere, calls it a night.

I contemplate laying back down with Colton. He looks so peaceful. I think for a moment about what the two of us would be like together. I don't allow myself to linger though. No point in daydreaming about something that won't ever happen.

I head to my room, set my alarm for four-thirty and fight to quiet my mind so I can get some sleep.

CHAPTER SIXTEEN

COLTON

After my ethics class, I hit the gym for a couple of hours before heading over to the cafeteria to meet up with the guys. We try to eat at least one meal a day together. It's become a sort of mandatory ritual; Coach thinks it'll help us come together and feel like a family.

I sit down at the table and pick at my food, which is crap by the way, but the dietician controls everything we eat during the season. The guys are talking about the upcoming game. As we get closer to the end of the regular season, the pressure to win every game increases. The practices have become more frequent, and we're constantly working on our offense and defense. We spend hours watching the tapes, and on top of that, we have to haul ass to make sure we don't fall behind academically.

This year, like the last, I'm determined to win.

It's crazy how great we were last year. Our team was the strongest it's ever been. We were legendary, and everyone is expecting the same this year, too. So far, we're delivering, but having most of the star players graduate wasn't the best way to start. Some fans blame the change in leadership, blame me for the shaky start and for playing too many close games, despite the fact that we've won them all.

"So, after every win, we throw a party," Zack says, bringing me back to the conversation.

"Seriously dude, we're going to be exhausted," Chase responds. A few of the guys nod in agreement.

"Nah, Zack's right. This is the motivation we need," Nick says. Of course my brother would support the idea of throwing a party.

"Guys, I don't think it's a good idea," I add, doing my due diligence even though I know they won't listen.

"What? Is your girl going to be mad that you're throwing parties and jersey chasers will be hanging all over you?" Matt, one of our kickers, asks.

"His girl wouldn't mind," Blake says, trying to help.

"Not his girl," Chase adds.

Like I need a reminder.

Zack winks. "Not yet."

When did my personal life become a topic of conversation?

"You guys will hate yourselves after every game. Trust me, if you play right, you'll be exhausted when you're done," I throw in, not bothering to respond to the comments about Mia. Maybe I should stop spending so much time with her. I dismiss the idea immediately. That's never going to happen. Not if I can help it.

"We'll play hard and party hard," Nick says from the other side of the table.

"Are we partying?" Kaitlyn asks from behind Nick. She's followed by Abbigail and her posse.

"Always, as long as you're there," Shane, a red-shirt freshman says to Kaitlyn. My eyes snap to him, and his widen in understanding. Out of the corner of my eye, I see Chase giving me the 'calm down' look.

All the girls find a seat with Kaitlyn taking her place next to Nick, and Abbigail sitting across the table from me.

"Okay, so it's settled—a party after every win," Zack says.

"After every game, because we're going to keep winning every game," Blake corrects.

"We'll throw a party at the house," Zack finishes, staring at me for confirmation.

"Whatever," I concede, but add, "I'm not going to help organize, or clean shit up."

"Not a problem, man, but you do need to be there."

"Yeah, wherever Hunter is, the ladies follow," Ian, a wide receiver, adds looking at Abbigail. Abbigail, who I feel is staring a hole through me while I do my best to ignore her.

I'm about to respond to Ian when I see Mia enter the dining hall.

"Fine, I'll be there," I say so they leave me alone. I don't want them to realize all my attention is on one person right now, on this one girl—scratch that—one woman. You would think that after seeing her in class yesterday, sleeping at her house last weekend while holding her in my arms, going to the gym with her, and having coffee with her every day this week, that I'd have had enough. Even seeing her tomorrow doesn't stop me from missing her whenever she's not around.

I tune out of the rest of the conversation though I pretend to listen. The guys are so into their discussion that they don't notice my attention is focused on the beautiful woman. I see her grab a burger and fries along with a drink. She stops, holding her tray in front of her, and looks around. Her eyes connect with someone across the room, then she smiles and waves. My head turns faster than lightning to see who put that smile on her face. Relief swarms me, jealousy leaving just as quickly, when I see it's Kiya waving back at Mia.

I turn back when I feel a foot ride up my leg, and I immediately glare at Abbigail. She clearly doesn't get that I want nothing to do with her. She's looking at me with a coy smile. Since she's still clueless, I'll do something that will make her understand. I shoot Blake a look and set everything in motion.

MIA

"Ugh, today sucked," I say the moment my tray hits the table.

"I bet my day was worse," Kiya challenges.

"That would suck for the both of us. Can we have a girl's night tonight to make it better?"

"Channing Tatum and Oreo shakes?"

That sounds heavenly. "You know me so well."

"It's what I do. Tell me what happened?"

"Long story. How much time you got?"

"Oh, shit, incoming."

"What—" Before I finish my question, I feel a hand land on my shoulder and a tray is placed next to mine. I don't have to ask who it is because my body already knows. I can feel it in the way my skin reacts to his touch. I can feel it in the tightening of my stomach.

Colton takes a seat next to me, and Blake sits next to Kiya. She looks at me, her eyes filled with a combination of shock and excitement. I don't even want to know what my face looks like right now.

Blake throws his arm around Kiya, and her face lights up. She may deny it, but she's falling for Blake. I can tell. And the way he looks at her shows he feels the same way. There's a long pause around the table, probably due to the unexpectedness of the guys joining us. Kiya, having more cojones than all of us combined, is the first to speak.

"What are guys like you doing in a place like this?"

I burst out laughing. My best friend is literally perfect. Blake follows my lead, and I can hear Colton chuckle.

"But seriously, what brings you here? Tired of hanging in the kingdom with the rest of the royals?" She points at the table filled with a bunch of larger-than-life guys, some even I recognize. I also notice Colton's sister is sitting there, and next to her is Abbigail, who is staring at us with something I can only label as disgust. Guess she won't be making her way to this table anytime soon.

I turn back and say, "Seems like you're already missed."

"That's all Hunter's," Blake says and my stomach drops with the reminder that she was once his.

"Not mine," Colton growls and I feel my knees buckle. If I weren't sitting down I'd likely do a repeat of the second day in class.

"Okay, okay. So, you guys are escaping the jersey chasers at your table then?" Kiya asks.

"Baby, you know I don't need an incentive to come to you," Blake says flirtatiously, pulling her in closer to his side.

She rolls her eyes, shoving him away gently. "Because you sit with me every day," she adds sarcastically.

"You never come to the dining room," he retorts and its true. Kiya apparently hates the dining room, and only came today because I texted her to meet me here for lunch. I wanted to tell her about how I got into a debate with my philosophy professor. In retrospect, it could have waited, but I feel like I barely see her anymore. Class, homework, study groups, and Blake have kept her busy and me ordering food.

"True, I'll give you that." She smiles and I'm a little jealous of their banter. Jealous of what they have, what they are, and what they can become. But I'm also extremely happy for Kiya. She deserves this and more.

"You don't come here often either," Colton says to me softly.

I give him a sideways glance. "I've met you here for lunch

before," I remind him and add "For all you know, I come here all the time."

"No, you don't. I would know."

"Doubt it. I'm not on your radar."

"Says who? I can tell the moment you step into a room."

I blush at his words. I know he's probably messing with me, but it doesn't stop me from feeling giddy.

Kiya and Blake start talking about their day, while Colton and I are happy to sit back and let them take the lead. Neither one of us is eager to speak. I still can't believe I shared a couch with him.

I take the last bite of my burger and I'm about to grab a fry when my hand runs into Colton's.

"Have you been eating my delicious fries?" I ask, dipping one into barbecue sauce.

"You just noticed? You've got to work on your situational awareness."

"Oh crap, Hunter. Never touch her food. It's the golden rule," Kiya says seriously.

"Why not?" he asks, grabbing another one of my fries.

"She's got a food obsession," my roommate says, preventing me from answering.

"I do not! You just didn't ask," I say pointing at her.

Colton leans in, whispering in my ear, "You're saying all I have to do is ask?"

"Yes," I reply breathlessly.

Wow, did it just get hot in here? It feels like we're no longer talking about fries.

"You never share your food with me," my roommate interrupts again.

I look away from Colton and shrug my shoulders. "You never ask."

"What are you doing tonight?" Blake asks Kiya, diverting the conversation.

"Oreo shakes and Channing Tatum," Kiya tells him nonchalantly.

"Doing Channing Tatum, huh?" Blake playfully lifts his eyebrows.

"Yeah, who wouldn't?" Kiya answers, and she's right. Even I wouldn't pass up on that, and that's saying a lot considering my virginity status.

"Will you share with me?" Colton asks.

"What? Oh." I push my fries to his side. Kiya scoffs from the other side of the table, but I just roll my eyes and smile.

"Blake and I will be there at eight," Colton says.

"Be where?" Kiya asks.

"At your place." Colton directs his answer to me, and then looks at Kiya.

"Wait, what?" I ask.

"Oreo shakes and movies sound like a great night," he adds like that's a proper answer.

"It's a girls' night. At least that was the plan," Kiya responds.

"Now it's just a night," Blake retorts, kissing her cheek.

"I can bring some food to pay you back for stealing your fries. Does that sound good?" Colton looks me dead in the eyes, waiting for a response, and I know my fries are not the only thing he's stealing from me.

"I guess that's okay," Kiya says seizing the opportunity.

"Thanks, babe. Can't wait." Blake kisses her cheek once more.

Well, there goes our girls' night and my venting about my professor.

"Shit, we've got to go. We're going to be late for practice," Blake says, shifting his focus from Kiya to Colton.

"Let's go." Colton grabs my now empty tray, places it on top of his, and walks to the trash can. I look in Kiya's direction, catching Blake leaning towards her for a kiss. I look away, trying to give them some privacy. When Colton comes back from dropping off the trays, he grabs his bag and looks at Blake, where I assume he catches the kiss I was trying to avoid.

He chuckles. "Get a room."

"Okay, let's go." Blake grabs his things.

"See you tonight then," Kiya tells him, trying to prolong their time.

"See ya," Blake gives her a quick peck.

I look back at Colton, startled to find him closer than I'd expected. He's close enough to kiss. And for the briefest moment, I think he's going to do exactly that. His hand glides along my cheek, and he places his mouth to my ear.

"I'd do the same if you let me," he whispers. My eyes flutter closed at his words, and when I open them back up, he's walking out the door.

"Not a word," I warn Kiya. I have no idea what that was about. If I'd let him do what, kiss me? Is that what he meant?

"Many words, but not now. I have class. Get ready to tell all later." She grabs her things and walks away.

I remain seated at the table, waiting for the erratic beating of my heart to cease.

The things he does to me with just words are incredible.

Someone clears their throat behind me. I turn, half expecting it to be Kiya so desperate to know what Colton whispered to me that she decided to skip class, but I'm completely wrong.

Instead, there are three sets of eyes on me; one of them filled with anger.

"Abbigail," I say, ready to get whatever is about to go down over and done with. "Kaitlyn," I add when I spot her standing behind Abbigail. She lowers her gaze, avoiding my eyes. I guess the lines have been drawn and I am the only one on my side at the moment.

"I was just stopping by to let you know that whatever you think might be happening with Colton, isn't," Abbigail says with a snarl.

For a second I want to tell her that it's really none of her business, but instead I go with the truth.

"There is nothing going on between Colton and me."

"You're damn right there isn't." She gets closer to me. I assume in an attempt to appear threatening or more intimidating. She's a couple of inches taller than me, and since I'm sitting down, she towers over me. I bet she enjoys feeling mighty.

I force myself to stop rolling my eyes. "I just said that."

"Understand, honey, that Colton is mine. So back off, or I'll make you back off."

Hers? Seriously. If he were hers she wouldn't have to be all in my face, warning me to back off. Pathetic. "Two things, *honey*. First, you don't scare me. I am *not* threatened by you. On the contrary, it seems you're threatened by me. Second, I don't think Colton would agree with you. He isn't property and he doesn't belong to you."

"You should be afraid. I can make your life really hard, sweetheart. Since you just got here, and you might not be aware, I'll tell you. I'm the one he always comes back to. Everyone knows that."

The blonde behind her nods in agreement, and I look to Kaitlyn, but she gives nothing away.

"Since I am new here, maybe I can teach you a little something about self-respect. Don't be the girl they always come back to. Be the one they never leave."

Seemingly irritated with me and the fact that I'm not backing down, she places her right hand on the table and leans in closer. I am hyper-aware, ready to strike if necessary.

"If you know what's good for you, you'll back off."

Tired of her petty threats, I get up from the table and grab my things. I turn my back to her and feel something cold and wet hit the back of my jacket.

"Oops," Abbigail says innocently as she tips her iced coffee all over me. Her blonde friend, the one standing next to Kaitlyn, laughs as the drink drenches my jacket and pants.

"I'm so sorry," Abbigail adds apologetically.

"Don't worry," I tell her mirroring her same fake ass smile. Two can play at that game. "I was going to take this off when Colton comes over tonight anyway."

Abby's nostrils flare suddenly. Oh, shit. I know I shouldn't have said that, but it just came out. I couldn't help it.

Abbigail's mouth opens and closes a few times, but nothing comes out. Behind her, Blondie's eyes look like they are ready to jump out of her face, and I think Kaitlyn's are dancing with excitement. Odd.

I guess my words shut Abbigail down since she just huffs and walks away. As she retreats, I hear her mutter the word, "bitch." I shake it off because I know it isn't true.

She leaves the dining hall and panic consumes me. Kaitlyn will surely tell her brother what I've insinuated. Ugh, I am so screwed.

Chapter Seventeen

MIA

The moment Kiya walks through the door, she demands to know what Colton had whispered in my ear.

"Was it something dirty? Did he bite your ear? Oh! Was it something so dirty you can't bear to repeat it to me?" she says, cornering me in the kitchen as I finish washing the dishes.

"Kiya, no!" I say, desperately trying to make her stop. "He just said he'd do the same if I let him."

My roommate frowns. "Do what, exactly?"

I shrug. "I don't know. You'll never believe what happened after that though." I tell her about my encounter with Abbigail.

"Is she kidding?" Kiya exclaims as I finish recounting the conversation. We move to the living room to organize it a little before the guys get here.

"I don't know. They did seem really close at the party." I remember the kiss they'd shared that night—the all too passionate kiss that made my stomach hurt.

"Word on the street is that's done with."

"What happened?" I ask, my curiosity getting the better of me.

"She got a little clingy, or so Blake says." My roommate grabs some of her coats from the rack and walks to her room.

"He's probably still sleeping with her though, right?" I yell as she retreats. I don't want her to confirm this, but I want to know if it's true. He probably told her no strings attached. He seems like the guy who wouldn't want anything or anyone holding him down.

"He's interested in someone else," Kiya says, smirking as she comes back into the room.

Of course he's into someone else. And here I thought he was into me.

"He's coming to see her today, actually," she adds, not letting me escape the conversation. I chuck a pillow at her.

"Shut up! I thought you were being serious." I tell her as I pick up some snack wrappers from the coffee table in front of the TV.

"I'm being serious, Mia. Colton volunteered to come over tonight." She wiggles her eyebrows at me. "And earlier today, he sat at our table."

Yep, monumental step he took there by sitting with the peasants.

I roll my eyes. "That doesn't mean anything," I respond.

"It does to everyone who's been worshipping the ground he walks on."

"Really, you think so?" I ask her because I want her to say yes. I want someone else to confirm what I have already been feeling.

"Yes, I do think so. Colton has never done that before."

"Never sat at a different table? Never hung out with friends and watched a movie? I'm pretty sure he's done that before." I roll my eyes again. At this point, they might permanently remain at the back of my head.

"Not really. He sticks with the guys on his team. Always. His group never changes and never allows any new members outside of new players."

"Abbigail is in it," I can't help but add.

"Only because of Kaitlyn, Mia. Colton likes you. He's never been like this before, never had to invite himself over to a girl's house. He's literally going out of his way to spend time with you. Everyone can tell, trust me. Why else do you think you're a blip on Abbigail's radar?"

I shrug.

"She felt threatened."

"Threatened, by me? If that's the case, she's mistaken. He is not interested in me. There has to be someone else." I insist on telling her the opposite of what I feel. Maybe I'm trying to convince myself that he couldn't possibly be interested in me.

"No, she's threatened by me," Kiya deadpans "Obviously by you, M! Maybe there's someone else, but he must not like her that much since he's coming here tonight to hang out with you instead."

"He's coming to hang out with us. With me, you, and Blake."

"Oh please. I've seen him God knows how many times over the last few years, and he's barely acknowledged my presence. I don't think he knew my name until after his party, and I think he only learned it because of you. He lives with Blake, too, which means he has no excuse to come here to hang out with him. He's coming here for you, M. I didn't peg you as the naïve type."

"Whatever," I say, not wanting to get any further into it. I wish I could agree with what Kiya is saying, but I can't. I can't bring myself to think that there is a possibility he might like me.

"Did you throw the popcorn in the microwave?" Kiya asks.

"Aren't they bringing food?"

"Yes, but we're watching a movie, so we need popcorn."

I'm not a fan of popcorn, not since working part-time at the movie theater when I was in high school. "We don't need it."

"Mia, put the damn popcorn in the microwave."

"Are you trying to impress Blake, Kiya? You seem edgy." I channel my inner psychologist. "Do you want to talk about it?"

"Are you trying to impress Colton?" she retorts.

"What would make you say that?" I ask her as I walk over to the kitchen.

"The fact that you aren't wearing your signature movie-watching-Frozen-pants," I hear her yell.

"I only wear those with you, dear. They're my special bonding with Kiya pants." There's no way I could wear those with other people around.

"Yeah, yeah. Is the popcorn popping?" she asks just as I place two bags of popcorn inside the microwave.

Coming back into the living room, I salute her. "Yes ma'am."

"What movie are we watching?"

"I don't know. Something with Channing Tatum," I say.

"Should we force the guys to watch *Magic Mike?*"

"Yes! That's the best idea. They deserve it for inviting themselves to our girls' night," I encourage her. I can already imagine the awkward and uncomfortable look on their faces when all the hotties start to dance and strip.

The doorbell rings, the little sound reverberating for a few seconds. Kiya runs to get the door while the microwave dings indicating the popcorn is ready. I head in the direction of the kitchen instead.

"Hi, babe," I hear Blake say.

"Hey," Kiya responds and I can imagine the smile on my roommate's face. "Hi, Colton," she adds, her tone a little more serious, and I laugh as I imagine her standing in front of Colton. He can be intimidating.

"She's in the kitchen. You know where that is," she says a little louder so that I hear it. She thinks she's funny.

"You need help?" Colton says seconds later as I'm taking out the bags of popcorn. I empty them into two bowls.

"No, I think I'm okay," I tell him while grabbing a bowl with each hand.

"Thanks for inviting us over," he says with a freaking breathtaking smile.

I smile back. "You sort of invited yourself."

"You could have said no. You can always say no," he says and I see self-doubt make a brief appearance.

"I didn't think I had a choice."

"You always have a choice."

Our conversation seems to be taking a serious turn. I clear my throat. "Well, I'm glad you're here. Kiya is stoked to be spending time with Blake."

"And you?"

"What about me?" I ask, knowing exactly what he means.

"Are you happy to be spending time with us? With me?" His eyes hold me in place as he waits for my response.

I blush. "Yes."

"We're starting the movie! Get in here," Kiya yells. Yelling has become her specialty, it seems.

"We better get in there," Colton says with a low chuckle and I almost melt. He takes a bowl from my hand, his fingers brushing mine in the process. Goosebumps break out all over my body. After a few seconds, he moves away, leaving my fingers tingling.

"Wait," I say remembering that I need to tell him about my interaction with Abbigail. Shit, this could ruin the rest of the night—maybe even ruin whatever this is between us. I've thought a million times about how to bring it up, or whether I should bring it up at all, but I know I have to – someone will. Time to come clean. I take a deep breath.

"What's up?" he asks.

"After you left the dining hall, Abbigail approached me…" I look down at my feet and start wiggling my toes.

"What did she want?" he practically growls.

"She was just marking her territory." Or trying to, anyway.

I can feel his anger rising, but I don't dare look at him. "I'm not her fucking territory."

"I figured you wouldn't like to be considered property, and I told her that. You don't look like the kind of guy that belongs to anyone."

"Did she say something to you? Do anything to you?" I can feel his eyes scanning my body. I assume he's looking to find any physical marks or signs of a cat fight.

"Nope. She wanted me to back off. She doesn't seem like the type to get down and dirty."

"You don't have to listen to her."

"I know I don't—not that she has anything to worry about anyway. But I did say something…"

Here it comes.

"What did you say?"

"She, uh, she purposefully dropped coffee on my shirt. And I—I told her I was planning to take it off when you came over tonight anyway, I'm sorry." Finally, I look up and meet his gorgeous eyes. They hold a hint of amusement, not the cloud of anger I expected.

"Why are you sorry?" he asks, smiling at me.

"Isn't it obvious? I think I gave her the wrong idea."

"You're saying she thinks there's something between us?" he says, pointing at me then to himself.

"Yeah." I look back down at the floor like it's the most interesting thing in the world.

"And is that what you wanted her to think?" he asks, closing the distance between us. Using his index finger, he lifts my chin, bringing my eyes to his once more.

"At the time I did," I admit.

"And why is that?" he says, his eyes holding what can only be described as desire. The tension in the air becomes palpable.

“Because…because I was upset. She threatened me.”

“Okay.”

“Okay?” I was not expecting that reply.

“Yes, okay,” he says, nodding.

“You’re all right with that? I implied you and I were… involved.”

He shrugs. “She cornered you and you fought back. I like that you stood up for yourself. You didn’t let her step all over you. Plus, it’s not like you lied.” Didn’t I though? We’re not really involved.

I’m just about to ask what he means when Blake’s voice interrupts me. “Can you two stop doing whatever it is you’re doing and get in the living room already?” Blake calls out. “The wings are getting cold and Kiya wants to start this movie!”

Colton and I walk into the living room, setting the popcorn on the coffee table. Kiya and Blake are sharing a couch, forcing Colton and me to do the same.

“You ready for some Channing Tatum?” Kiya asks and I join her laughing.

“Are we really watching Magic Mike?” Blake complains as Kiya chooses the movie from our library and presses play.

“You chose to intrude on girls’ night. Now you must face the consequences.”

The guys grunt their disapproval and the movie begins.

We make side comments, eat wings, and popcorn for the rest of the night. Colton gets closer to me, then starts drawing circles on my thigh, my wrist, and the side of my stomach with his index finger.

Cue the butterflies and goosebumps.

I try to focus on the movie and Channing’s gorgeous body, but it’s impossible when Colton is distracting me with his touch.

Chapter Eighteen

MIA

Zack places his pen down with an audible slap. "Do we have to do homework? It's the weekend. The girls, booze, and parties are calling my name."

We're at the Football House, hiding out down in the basement. According to Colton, it's the only part of the house yet to be contaminated by the pigs he lives with.

"Yes, Zack. We have to. It's the last thing we have to do before the draft for the final paper is due," I tell him, trying to encourage him.

"It's not like you've been present for anything else," Colton adds.

"It's not like you minded," Zack retorts and I instantly blush.

"Okay boys, settle down. We've gotten our sources and we've interviewed Zack's parents. All we have to do is submit an outline before the final part." Groans follow my statement and I roll my eyes.

"You say it like it's easy," Zack says.

"Aw, you afraid you aren't smart enough?" I tease hoping to motivate him to do something. Although Zack is kind of flakey, I understand why now. After the semi-fight with Colton about whose parents to interview, we agreed to interview Zack's. He put up a bit of a fight when we told him, but since he was the absentee party, he had no choice but to comply. It also helped that we told him he'd become the horrid group member no one wants because they do no work.

During the interview, I found out that Zack's parents are factory workers who live in Massachusetts. They've been scraping by. Zack was a surprise for them, but from the interview, I could tell they adored him by the way they spoke about him. I can tell he loves them, too.

They told us Zack goes to visit as often as he can, and helps them out financially by working part-time at a store stacking shelves. Zack was a little embarrassed by this, and if he could have stopped his parents from telling us, he might have. But they were too proud of him not to share.

I hate to say it, but that was not what I was expecting. Serves me right for judging. I mean he's also a cocky, red-haired, six-foot-two football player. It goes to show there's always more to someone.

When we talked to his parents about our topic, they seemed baffled. They just couldn't understand how a parent could betray their child in that way. They love Zack so much and couldn't imagine hurting him. I felt a pang of jealousy; I wish I had that.

"You know I'm smart enough, babe."

"Can we get started now?" Colton interrupts.

"Yes, sir. How do you want to split it?" I ask since he seems to be giving orders.

"We have three main focus areas, right?"

"Yes, we have the first part where we discuss what's going on now, what the problem is and how many people it affects," I tell him.

"We have the 'why should you care' part, which is pretty self-explanatory," Colton adds, picking up where I left off.

"Yeah, and we also have the 'how can you help?' section, which is the solution—the whole point of this paper," I explain.

"Okay, so the last part is basically the purpose of this whole assignment?"

"Yeah, that's what I just said, Zack. For someone who claims to be smart, you're falling behind."

"I was just confirming it, sweetheart."

"Task at hand," Colton interrupts again.

"Yes, sir," Zack replies with a smirk.

Colton says something under his breath, but it was so low I don't hear it. He continues, "Let's each choose a section and outline every point within it. Then we'll rotate so we get to review each other's part and make sure we don't miss anything. That good?"

"You're the boss," Zack salutes him.

"Taking charge, I see," I add, unable to help myself from adding wood to the fire. Messing with Colton is fun.

"I always take charge," he responds in a firm, sexy voice, and it feels like the tables have turned. Now I'm the one on the spot, and I can feel the blush creeping in.

"Should I leave the room?" Zack mocks, unintentionally saving me from having to answer.

"Stay in the room for now," Colton replies. "I'll let you know when we're ready for you to head out." He flashes Zack a cocky smile.

I swat him on the shoulder, although I want to punch him instead for insinuating that we would need a room.

"If you ever want to share, let me know," Zack adds, and I feel like I'm invisible again. A whole conversation about me taking place, and I'm not a party to it.

"Fuck no. I don't share what's mine," Colton growls. It's a caveman reaction, and it makes me want to be his.

"I'll take part three," I say, diverting the whole conversation.

"Okay, I'll do part one. Zack, you should do part two. Not going to be hard telling people why they should care about human sex trafficking of children."

"Will do," Zack says, marking the end of our discussion. We all grab our computers and get to work.

"That was productive," I say to Colton as he drives me home. This has become pretty normal—me sitting in the passenger seat of Colton's car, music playing in the background. Twice a week, we meet up to work on the final paper. Colton insists on picking me up and dropping me off each time in addition to picking me up for coffee every morning. Tonight, the sound of raindrops crashing into the windshield accompanies the sounds of the music.

"It was. We're almost done with it."

"Yeah, just the writing part is left."

"And the presentation."

"Yes, that. How could I forget." I shudder at the thought of standing in front of everyone.

He keeps driving and we fall into a comfortable silence. Comfortable; that's how I feel when I'm with him.

"I told you, you don't have to drop me off every time," I say breaking the silence. "You also don't have to pick me up either. I have functioning legs that could use the workout."

"First, it's raining. Second, your legs are perfect as they are. Trust me," he says, and I smack his shoulder playfully.

"Third," he says, his eyes briefly connecting with mine before returning to the road. "I will pick you up and drop you off whenever the hell I want."

"I don't think so, and chill it with the caveman response."

I laugh at his ridiculous statement, yet inside, I melt over how possessive he can be.

"Plus, you're coming over to my place. When you do that, it just makes sense for me to pick you up and drop you off," he says.

"I've offered up my place." And I have, but he doesn't take me up on it often.

"We do study at your place, but when Zack is with us, I'd rather we do it at mine."

"That makes no sense."

"It makes sense to me. Zack doesn't need to get any ideas."

Any ideas about what? I wonder. Maybe having Zack come to my place might make him think there's something going on between Colton and I. Colton wouldn't want that.

"Okay," I say, ignoring the cracks I feel appearing in my heart.

"I'm not done."

"That was three reasons."

"Who cares? I have more."

I chuckle at his enthusiasm to speak. Initially, I'd pegged him as a man of few words. "Okay, go on."

"It's not safe for you to walk alone so late at night. I like knowing you're safe."

"I can text you when I get home."

"I would worry while I wait. This way is better. I get to witness it."

"I can manage, Colton. It's not your job to protect me."

"Might not be my job, but I'll do it anyway."

I roll my eyes. "You do know after this assignment is submitted, I will still be walking myself to places. And I will have to be responsible for my own safety and protection." I say it like it's nothing, like I expect us to drift apart. But just the thought of it makes my chest hurt. I've been living in a bubble, and I know that soon enough, I'll have to step out of it.

"Wow, are you saying you're only with me for this project? I thought we were more than just a forced assignment," he scoffs, and while I know he's being extra dramatic, I'm relieved he isn't thinking about discarding me the moment this assignment is out of our hands.

"Just figured you'd get sick of me, and want an out. I thought you were biding your time."

"You haven't been bad company, Mia. I don't think I could get sick of you."

"I can say the same about you."

"So, back to my point. I don't want you walking places at night on your own. I'll allow it during the day if I must, but any other time, just call me. I'm only a phone call away."

"'Allow me'? Very funny. And what, you'll come running to my aid? My knight in shining armor?"

"You're no damn damsel in distress, but I won't complain about you considering me your knight." I smile because he has been like my knight. He's been spending all of his free time with me. He's always caring, stealing touches, and glances whenever he can. I can't help but think maybe Kiya was right. Maybe Colton does care about me as more than a friend—care about me in the way I find myself caring about him.

"Thanks for the ride. I guess I appreciate not walking in the rain," I say the moment the car pulls into the driveway.

"Like I'd ever let you do that." He says as his hand twists the key in the ignition, shutting off the engine. We both sit in silence, neither one of us making a move or saying a thing. I guess I'm the one that's supposed to move, but I don't want to. So, I sit back and listen to the rain.

"I'd better go," I eventually say, taking off my seatbelt.

"Wait," he says, and I think he's going to ask me to stay, or say something. Instead, he takes off his seatbelt, opens his door and comes around to my side of the car, opening the door.

"You know you didn't have to open the door. I get it. You have manners, but it's raining. You're getting wet!"

Colton chuckles. "I think only you can do that." At his words, I'm consumed with embarrassment. I can't believe he just went there. If it weren't for the cold rain falling down on us, he'd probably be able to feel the heat emanating from my body.

He walks me to my door, where we stand on the last step just looking at each other.

He lifts his right hand to move a wet strand of hair that has become stuck to my forehead, and places it behind my ear.

Suddenly, the rain, which had been lightly falling, begins to pick up speed. I close my eyes getting lost in the sound, the feel of the cold water, and the peace that spreads through my body.

I feel Colton get closer, and I open my eyes to find him mere inches away. I suck in a breath as he cups my face, bringing us closer still. In a matter of seconds, his lips touch mine, and my eyes close once more. His lips continue their exploration, gently at first, and then unyieldingly hard. I feel myself falling—not just physically, but emotionally too.

I open for him and his tongue snakes its way inside my mouth. His hands move from my face to my lower back as he pulls me toward him, closing whatever space was left between us. He pushes me against my front door as he deepens the kiss. One of his hands remains on my hip, while the other travels the length of my side, and settles on the side of my neck. He presses our lips closer together, holding on to me like I'm his lifeline.

My right leg moves of its own volition, hiking up towards Colton's hips, desperate for friction. The hand that was on my hip moves, supporting my leg as he presses into me.

No thought, or dream could ever come close to how it feels having Colton's lips on mine—to have him kiss me like this. No kiss I've ever experienced has ever made my heart beat faster.

A soft whimper escapes my lips, and Colton growls in response. We finally come up for air, and while breathing is good, I'd rather have his lips back on mine.

"That was…" Colton stops midsentence, and I nod in agreement. No words could describe the electricity I felt the moment our lips touched.

"Want to come inside?" I don't want him to go—not yet. I've had a taste and now I need more.

"I don't think that's a good idea," he responds, and the feeling of rejection overcomes me. How could he kiss me like that, and then reject me so easily? Maybe he regrets the kiss, and now I've made a fool of myself by inadvertently showing him how much I liked it. I look away.

"Mia." He lifts my chin with his finger and directs his piercing gaze at me. "I want to come inside, but I don't think I'd be able to stop myself if I did. You deserve more," he says, but all I can think about is whether he's telling me he's incapable of giving me more, not that I've asked him to.

"So, I'll pick you up at seven-thirty tomorrow night," he says.

"Why?" I ask.

"Because I'm giving you more." I'm a little confused. It's probably because he kissed me silly. "I'm taking you out tomorrow," he says.

"Out?"

He smiles and shakes his head. "On a date, Mia."

He wants to take me out on a date?

"I'll see you tomorrow," he says, not waiting for me to agree. Well, I guess it's a good thing he never asked, just stated. His lips come crashing into mine once more and I'm captivated by him, consumed by the softness of his lips and the strength of his kiss.

He pulls away again, bites his lip, and walks back to his car. I wave goodbye, open the door, and let myself into the house. My mind races, trying to make sense of tonight. I close the door, walk to the window, watch Colton's car pull out of my driveway and disappear from sight.

I bring my index finger to my lips, feeling how swollen they are, wanting to commit tonight to memory—not that I could ever forget. I start counting the hours until his car will reappear in my driveway, and I get to see him once again.

Chapter Nineteen

COLTON

My phone buzzes in my pocket as I get into the car to go and pick up Mia. She's letting me take her out on an actual date tonight. Not that our coffee and study dates aren't great, but I want more time with her. Just Mia and I, no assignment and no Zack. I want more time to focus on her almond-shaped eyes, on her perfect smile, on the way she blushes when I watch her.

My phone buzzes again. I look at the caller ID, and I'm immediately consumed with rage.

"What do you want?" I spit out.

"Now there, honey, that's not the way to greet your mother now, is it?"

Right, mother, I think bitterly. Like she's earned that right.

"What do you want, Adaline?"

"Oh, sweetie, I'd change my tone if I were you," she says threateningly.

I sigh, resigned to my position. "Did you need something?" I ask, changing my tone into something more neutral.

"Yes, I did. I'm throwing together a family dinner tonight. I expect you and the others to be here at eight. Don't be late."

She must have realized that her charade wouldn't keep, that her image as the perfect mother would be tainted if she didn't hold mandatory dinners. It might actually wake my father up and get him to start wondering why his kids never come to the house. It's not like we live hours away; it's only a fifteen-minute drive.

"I have plans."

"You do. You have a family dinner."

I don't hold back the snarl. "That's not what I meant."

"Call the others. I'll see you then. And Colton?" she says, "Don't be late."

I slam my hand on the steering wheel. In two minutes, my mother has managed to screw everything. I get out of my car, slamming the door behind me, and walk back into the house. I find the nearest coffee table and slam it against the wall. I wish it were my fists connecting with it instead but I can't. Watching the table is a great distraction from the anger that's brewing within me.

I grab my phone and shoot Mia a quick text, telling her I can't make it. I call Kaitlyn and let her know we've been summoned. Then, I run upstairs to Nick's room and tell him the same. Nick and Kaitlyn's reaction, contrary to mine, is one of excitement. They're happy to spend time as a family. They'll take whatever crumbs our parents give them.

The idea of a family dinner sounds great to them, and like death row to me. It's funny how most parents would be ecstatic to have their kids want to spend time with them, while mine are too distracted, too busy, too fucking deceitful to care.

I'm still tempted to punch the wall, but decide against it. I have two shots at complete freedom and one of them requires I have a decent throwing arm. That includes my ability to hold the ball with my hand. Instead, I grab a beer from the kitchen, gulping it down in one go. I hope it helps shrink the lump that has lodged itself in my throat, but I know it won't. This is something that won't go away until the truth is revealed.

With Mia, I forget that I carry this load, but the feeling comes right back when I'm not with her. It feels like at some point, the weight will inevitably crush me.

Nick and I pull into our parents' driveway a few minutes later, the memories from that day rushing back like they're being chased. I've rarely stepped into this house since then. I haven't wanted to, haven't needed to, but here I am.

Kaitlyn pulls up next to us as I shut off the car. I get out, wanting to get this over with. All I have to do is play a role, pretend to be a family just long enough to make it through dinner.

Shit, I can't believe I'm stuck here when I could be with my girl.

MIA

I get out of the shower and step into my room. My clothes, which took me two hours to choose, are laid out on the bed. I've had this stupid smile plastered on my face since Colton asked me on a date. A real date! Cue the music and twirling around like a princess that has just found her prince. Seriously, cheesiest imagery, but it depicts exactly how I'm feeling at this very moment.

I'm shaking my butt to the most upbeat music I could find. I've gone all out for this date – hair soon to be done, nails done, everything done. I felt the occasion called for it. An incoming text message interrupts my music. I set down the wand, and move to my nightstand. Colton's name is on the screen, and I unlock the phone to open the message, excited to see what he has to say.

'Can't make it. Raincheck?'

That's all it says—four words that instantly sour my mood. I turn off the wand, put my clothes away, and change the song. I'm not feeling fancy anymore—just stood up.

"This calls for another date with Channing Tatum," I say out loud to no one. I throw on my go-to Frozen pants, and a t-shirt, ready to be as comfortable as I can. Kiya and Blake are out tonight, which likely means she won't be coming back to the house.

Crap. It's been a while since I've spent a Saturday night alone in my apartment. I've spent the last God knows how many Saturdays hanging out with either Kiya or Colton or both. Even Zack and Blake sometimes become part of the group. It's crazy how much things have changed in the last couple of months. Saturday nights alone watching TV used to be my refuge—something I'd look forward to at the end of a hectic week. But now I look forward to something entirely different.

As I sit on the couch, settling in for a night to myself, I can see how much of me I've already given to Colton, despite my attempts to hold back. He consumes my thoughts from the moment I wake until I go to sleep. It serves me right. He canceled on me thirty minutes before he was supposed to pick me up like it was nothing. I guess it doesn't mean as much to him as it does to me.

He says raincheck.

I say reality check.

Chapter Twenty

COLTON

"How's school been?" my father asks, completely clueless as to what's been going on in our lives. Nick and Kaitlyn start telling him about their classes. Kaitlyn thinks one of her professors hates her. She whines and complains about her sorority, and how some of her sisters are petty. Nick jokes about going to too many parties and having his pick of girls. At least dad thinks he's joking. I know he isn't.

"That's wonderful, darling," Adaline says in a sweet manufactured tone after Nick and Kaitlyn finish updating them on their lives.

A guttural sound escapes my mouth without me being able to control it. I grab the beer I've been nursing since this dinner started and finish it in one draw. It's not enough to get me through this charade unscathed, but it's what I have. I can't drink anything more, though. I need to be able to drive myself out of here if need be.

"Everything okay, Colt?" my dad asks. I guess he's finally noticed my discomfort.

"He's fine. Just being his usual grumpy self," my mother answers before I can.

"You would know," I mutter under my breath.

"What was that?" my dad asks again, clueless as always.

"Ignore him," Adaline cuts me off. I guess she's afraid of what I may say. She should be.

"Anyway," Kaitlyn says, sensing the shift in the mood. The tension is so thick you can cut it with a knife.

"Dad, your birthday is coming up! You're going to be an old man," my brother jumps in after Kaitlyn.

"Better with age," Dad responds, and I feel bad for him.

"Handsome as ever," Adaline adds.

"Fuck this," I say, pushing the chair from under me and sending it scraping along the floor.

"Colt, where are you going?" my dad asks, and I pity him. His nose is so deep in work that he forgets to look around and see what's right in front of his face. I don't respond, turning from them.

"Colton Hunter, sit back down!" Adaline screeches like a pathetic child stomping her foot when she isn't getting what she wants.

Fuming, I disregard her command and saunter toward the living room, desperate to get outside and leave this place. If I don't ever return, it'll be too soon.

"Come back here before you regret it!"

"I do regret it! Every day!" I shout back, turning to face her. "Do *you?*"

My father follows me into the living room. "What do you mean?"

I see Kaitlyn and Nick on their feet confusion visible on their faces. They don't know why I'm acting like this, and if they did, they'd understand. Not just that, but they would be running out of here too.

"Just ignore him," Adaline says, standing beside my father and interlocking her fingers with his.

"Yes, please. Go ahead and do what you've been doing for the last couple of years. Ignore what's right in front of you!" I yell back, and although I pity my father, I also blame him. He should have paid more attention.

"Colton Hunter!" my mother screams, like the level of her voice might make me change my mind. I've kept quiet long enough, and while I know that I can't say what I want to say, I also won't sit here and pretend to be the perfect family.

I hightail it out of there, get in my car and speed off. My blood is boiling. I'm so angry I can see red. Without realizing it, I've stopped my car outside Mia's house, my mind telling me that I need to be with her. Somehow, she's become my ultimate destination, the only person who can help me deal.

I park on the curb, staring up at Mia's illuminated living room window. I can't see her like this though; I'm still so fucking angry. She deserves better—so much better. I know she's too good for me, but I'm too selfish to let her go.

I glance around, spotting a bar close by. One drink would take the edge off. One drink to make the anger subside. One drink and then I can see Mia.

My Mia.

MIA

A loud knock startles me awake, and I almost fall off the couch. I really need to stop falling asleep in the living room. I hesitantly get up and head to the door. Kiya's probably forgotten her keys.

I open it to find Colton looking back at me.

"You need to ask who it is before opening the door," he says, slurring his words. I can smell the Jack on his breath, and the memories it brings are not pleasant ones.

I cross my arms. "Hi to you too." Who the hell does he think he is showing up at my doorstep drunk after canceling our date and trying to tell me what to do?

"I'm serious, Mia. What if it had been a thief? Or someone worse?" he sternly says.

"It wasn't, so there." I puff out my chest and maintain eye contact, daring him to say anything else. I should be the one upset with him. I wasn't the one who bailed tonight. He was. If anyone should be asking questions, it should be me.

"It could have been."

"Yes, Colton. It could have, but it wasn't." I sigh and slowly begin closing the door. I can't deal with a wasted Colton right now. After tonight, I don't even know whether I'd like to deal with a sober Colton either.

"Wait, what are you doing?" He holds the door, preventing me from shutting it in his face.

"I'm going to bed. You're drunk. I'm upset. I don't think we'd have the best conversation right now." I attempt to shut the door again, but his arm doesn't give.

"I'm sorry I canceled our date at the last minute," he says, his gaze holding me in place.

"I don't know if I am," I respond and I mean it. I've gotten too close to the heat and today was likely a warning that I should back up before I get burned.

"What do you mean?"

"I mean, I'd rather have this conversation when you're sober."

"Don't shut me out, Mia. Please. Let me in?" he asks and the problem is I already have. He looks pleadingly at me and I move away from the door, heading to the couch again.

"You're watching *Magic Mike* again?"

"He kept me company tonight while someone I was supposed to go out with bailed last minute." I eye him suspiciously. "And apparently partied somewhere else." I know my tone is accusatory, but I can't help it.

"That guy sounds like an asshole," he says with a small smirk.

I keep it short and ignore the effect his smile has on me. "Yup."

"He's sorry."

"Sorry he asked me out? Sorry he bailed? Why are you here anyway?" I put all my questions out there at once. Let's get this over with.

"Not sorry I asked you out, trust me. I'd rather have been with you than where I was. And, I'm here because I had to deal with some shit, and you were the only person I wanted to see after—the only person I wanted to talk to."

His words start melting the wall I had spent the last few hours building.

"Did the crap you had to deal with involve getting hammered?"

"I… Shit this looks bad, but I needed something to numb me be… before… before I came to see you."

Ouch.

I don't have a poker face, so Colton must see how I'm feeling and adds, "I wanted to be less angry when I showed up at your place."

"Are you angry with me?"

"Never. I'm angry at everyone else." He sits next to me on the couch, our legs pressed against one another, leaving no space between us. I can sense he wants to talk to me, but I don't push him. I know he'll share with me when he's ready.

"I was at my parents' tonight," he says, kicking off his shoes. He lays on his back and places his head in my lap, resuming the same position as the last time we'd talked about parents.

Instinctively, I start playing with his hair.

"I was getting ready to pick you up when Adaline called."

"Adaline?" I ask, feeling both curious and jealous.

"My mother," he answers. He says 'mother' like it hurts to push that word out, to call her that. I look down at him, seeing the tension in his jaw. I caress his face and watch his eyes close and then open once more.

"She called about a last-minute family dinner and I couldn't say no."

"It makes sense. You'd want to take advantage of spending time with your family. I see why you would feel like you couldn't say no."

"No," he says tightly. "I didn't want to go. I never do. And even less so when I already had plans with you. But I can't say no."

"Okay," I wonder why he feels like he can't say no.

"Can I trust you?"

I can hear the vulnerability in his voice. I see his eyes searching mine for an answer.

"Yes," I say softly, confirming what he already knows. If he thought he couldn't trust me, he wouldn't have said anything. "But you don't have to. You don't have to tell me anything you—"

"I want to. I need to," he says, cutting me off. Seeing him laying down on my lap like this, asking me to listen to him shows me a whole different side of him—one I knew was lying beneath the surface, but many don't get to see. It's difficult for him, but he's trying to let me in, trying to let me help him, and I want nothing more than to help push away the shadows clouding his eyes. And while they are still beautiful, I know they hold pain. A lot of pain. Because I know that look. It's the same look I sometimes have, yet work so hard to hide.

He takes in one giant breath. "I walked in on my mother having sex with another man," he says, spitting the words out as quickly as he can.

"I'm so…" I don't finish the sentence because he doesn't need or want my pity. All he wants is someone to talk to, someone that won't judge him. "Did you tell anyone?" I ask.

"Yeah, you," he says, and I immediately realize the weight he's been carrying and how strong he is for carrying it alone. The physical strength he has fades in comparison. I continue playing with his hair, trying to comfort him. I try and give him whatever strength I can spare, whatever he needs.

"Does she know?"

"Oh, she knows," he says bitterly. His anger is returning, and I know that this conversation killed the buzz he came in with. His words are coherent, and his eyes are clearer.

"Not only does she know, but she won't let me tell anyone," he adds.

"How can she stop you?"

"She's a… she said Nick and Kaitlyn are not my dad's biological kids."

If I had a glass in my hand, it would have dropped and shattered.

"She told me if I said anything, she'd tell dad and he'd kick them out. I can't do that to Nick and Kaitlyn. They've suffered enough by having a shitty mother, and a father who's always too busy. If Dad finds out, he might stop paying for their schooling. They won't graduate, they won't finish their degrees, and they'll probably spiral out of control—more than they already have. I just can't put them through this," he says.

I feel a pain in my chest. His pain has somehow become mine and my heart breaks for him.

"You think she's telling the truth?" I ask, hoping she could be lying. I know a thing or two about horrible parents, but how a mother can threaten her own child with ruining the life of her other kids just doesn't fit in my head.

"I don't know, but it's too risky to call her bluff."

"You're … amazing," I say, voicing my thoughts.

"I'm not."

"Yes, you are."

"No, Mia. I'm a coward."

"You're watching out for your brother and sister. They're lucky to have you."

He rolls his eyes dismissing my comment. I can't believe he doesn't realize the strength it takes to shield everyone else from the bullets while taking the hits.

"So, Adaline called today and summoned us all for dinner. She tried to have us behave like a happy family, and I couldn't fucking do it," he continues.

"Did you tell them?" Maybe that's why he showed up looking so unlike the put together Colton we all see.

"I almost did, but instead I walked out like the coward I am," he says again, and I know he believes it.

"You're not," I insist, knowing it's falling on deaf ears.

"So, I drove and drove and ended up outside your apartment. I walked to a bar and had a few drinks and then came back to you. Because you give me strength," he says, grabbing the hand I was using to play with his hair and bringing it to his lips. He kisses every fingertip slowly, and I know it's his way of thanking me for listening.

"Colton," I say, trying to bring him back. I know he feels exposed after talking to me. I know he wants a distraction.

"Hmm?" he says between kisses.

"Colton."

He lifts himself up and captures my lips in a kiss. I want to return it, but I know I shouldn't—not right now.

"Please," he whispers, sensing my hesitation. The vulnerability in his eyes reels me in and I kiss him back fervently. Our lips devour one another. I put it all in the kiss, hoping that through it, I can show him I'm here for him. I kiss him hoping that two people who have been broken by life can help put each other back together.

We spend the rest of the night laying on the couch, watching movies and kissing. Neither one of us says anything else. We've said enough for one night.

Chapter Twenty-one

MIA

"It's boring," I say, unlocking the front door. Colton and I have just come back to my place after going to play mini golf. I told him last week that I'd never gone golfing, and he was appalled. And, because it's still winter, we had to settle for the kiddy version.

"You're breaking my heart, Mia."

"You'll get over it."

"I don't know. This might be the end of us."

"Hmm, have we even begun?" I ask, letting us into my bedroom. We decided that the living room was not the right place for us after Kiya caught us asleep and cuddling yet again. I think Kiya has enough photographic evidence now to extort us at some point. So, I got a TV and put it in my room, and that's where Colton and I have our movie marathons…well, where we pretend to watch movies.

"You know we've begun," he says, kissing me and biting my bottom lip. I kiss him back, so incredibly happy I'm able to do this whenever I want. Ever since that first kiss, we've been unable to stop.

The kiss becomes more passionate, more intense. Colton lifts me up and sits on my bed so I'm straddling him. He kisses me like he's dying of thirst. One of his hands is buried in my hair, while the other moves all over my body, feeling me over my clothes. His tongue dances inside my mouth and I match his every move. His breathing becomes heavy, erratic and the friction we're creating causes a moan to escape me. Pulling his lips from mine, he moves his hands from my hair to my shirt. In one rapid motion, he pulls it off and throws it across the room. His lips are back on me in record time, his hands expertly undoing my bra.

I feel it come undone, and he switches our positions so my back is to the bed and he's lying on top of me. That's when red flags start waving.

"Colton," I say, breaking the kiss and touching his arm to halt his movements.

"Yes?" he says, his eyes glazed with lust. He leans in to kiss me again, but I bring up my palm, creating a barrier between us.

"Colton, I think we should stop," I repeat. "I'm not having sex with you."

He immediately rolls over to the side of the bed, freeing me from under him. "Shit, I'm sorry," he says, scrubbing his face with his hand.

I sit up, missing the feel of his body on mine. "It's not that I don't want to," I say, trying to explain.

"I understand, Mia. It's too soon," he says, his hand caressing my side.

I take a deep breath. "Colton, I—"

"You don't need to explain. I'm sorry I pushed you."

"You didn't push me, trust me. I wanted to. I *want* to. I just want my first time to be special," I say, laying back down and turning on my side to meet his eyes.

"Your first time with *me?"* he asks.

I look up at the ceiling. "No, my first time," I answer.

"You're a..."

"Virgin, yes. I promised myself that when it happens it would be meaningful, and with someone I saw myself spending the rest of my life with. I was kind of saving myself for marriage," I spit out.

There's never a proper time for this conversation, but this is as good a time as any. It's better to have him run out the door now than before I'm in too deep.

Who am I kidding, though. I'm already there.

"It's silly, I know," I say feeling my cheeks heat up. I try to turn to the opposite side of the bed, but Colton stops me.

"Mia." He takes my chin and lifts it. I avert my eyes, again ready for this to be the end of us.

"I'm sorry I didn't tell you earlier." I motion between us. "This is rather new."

"Mia." He tries to make eye contact again, but I avoid him.

"So, now you know you shouldn't date me. I can't give you what you want." I'm waiting for him to get up and leave, but he doesn't move. I start getting up from the bed, but he holds my hips and pulls me back down.

"I can get sex from anyone," he says, and I roll my eyes. There's the conceited ass I met the first time, and it hurts a little because I know he's telling the truth. I know there's a line of girls out there who would trample each other for the chance to be with him. Shit, I've seen it first hand with Abbigail.

"What I mean is—Mia look at me."

I don't.

"Look at me. Now!" At his comment, I obey. "Mia, if all I wanted was sex, I'd go to anyone else. There are plenty of willing girls."

Yep, thanks for the reminder.

"Perfect. Go and find one of them. Maybe Abbigail?" I say, and it feels like I'm swallowing rusty nails. "I'm sure she'd—" I'm stopped when Colton kisses me.

"Shut up, and listen," he says. "You don't need to give me sex to give me what I need. You give me strength, you listen to me, and you're there when I need you. You allow me to be me, and inspire me to be a better version of myself."

"You can get that from me as a friend," I counter. "You should date someone—"

Again, his lips on mine stop me from finishing my suggestion.

"I want you, Mia, and I can wait. But I won't give you up."

"You'll want to have sex."

"Yeah, I will. I do right now, but not with just anyone. I want it with you, and if that means waiting, I'll do so. Gladly. But I don't want anyone else, and you don't want me with anyone else. So, quit suggesting stupid shit," he says, and I smile. I feel like I'm walking on air. I didn't expect this to be his reaction.

"Are you sure?" I ask, giving him another chance to get out.

"If I wasn't sure, I wouldn't be here right now. Don't call it quits before we've even started, okay, Collins?"

"Yes, Hunter," I respond and kiss him.

We watch another movie, but really that's just an excuse for us to make out while the movie plays in the background. We get under the sheets and kiss until I'm too tired to continue. I begin to drift off, thinking about how the last few weeks have felt like a dream, and I'm a little afraid to wake up and find it all gone. Maybe this can work out after all. That's the last thought that crosses my mind before I give in to the sleep that beckons me.

There!

I look at myself in the mirror, checking out my ironed curls. A couple of months ago, I wouldn't have bothered primping and preening to go to a party. Shit, Kiya would certainly agree with that. She'd have forced me to go in the first place, and then we'd fight about getting ready. Yet here I am, curling my hair and perfecting my makeup.

There is a key difference now; I have someone I care about—the same someone who was here immediately after his game ended today in his amazing uniform that hugs his form beautifully. Even after playing for a couple of hours, he still made time to see me, to kiss me and let me know they'd won.

We haven't put a label on whatever the heck is going on between us. We're with each other whenever we can be, though, which isn't a lot nowadays since his games have been taking up more and more of his time.

He wanted to stay for longer, but needed to get his sweaty ass over to the house to help the guys set up for the party they have each time they win. They've had one every Saturday because they're kicking ass.

I slide on a jacket and take another look in the full-length mirror to make sure I look okay. Even though he was only here a couple of hours ago, I can't help but feel giddy about seeing him again.

I grab my purse, the kind I throw on my shoulder and cross to the side, and leave the room. Kiya got held up in a study group session so she won't be joining me until much later. It feels a little weird to be going to a party by myself, but I promised Colton I'd be there.

I open the front door and run right into someone I didn't ever expect to see again.

My father.

Time stops as I try and figure out if this is a dream or not—if my dad is actually standing in front of me after months and months of not seeing him. If the same person who abandoned me is the one standing at my door.

"Hey, kiddo," he says. That voice—I haven't heard it since I heard mom and dad argue in the kitchen. I don't reply. "I know you're mad at me, and I understand."

"Well, if you understand, that makes it all better," I say, my words clipped.

"I know it doesn't, but I'm here."

"Yeah. Please tell me why you're here."

"I want to apologize," he says, his sky-blue eyes looking back at me.

"For what, exactly?" I respond, going through the list of all the things he did wrong.

"For everything. I needed to come here and apologize to you."

"Now? How did you even know I was here?"

"Yes, now, and I asked CU and they told me you'd transferred. I'm your father so they gave me the information."

"Father? Really?" I throw back in disgust. "You're claiming that now?"

"I deserve that too, but I just want you to know, I'm better now."

I don't believe a word he's saying. "Are you?"

"I am," he says solemnly. "Will you please let me come inside so we can talk?"

I stand there blocking the door for a couple of minutes before I acquiesce. Part of me knows he's my father, and I was taught to respect that. I move away and let him follow me in. I find my comfy spot on the couch and wait for him to start talking, to try and explain what happened.

"I know I've made some mistakes." Instead of following me to the couch, Michael walks around the living room, stopping in front of a photo of Mom and me.

"You take after her, you know? Just like her," he adds.

"I'd like to think so. You were saying you made some mistakes?"

I tell him, trying to move this conversation along.

"Many mistakes, but I'm better. After your mom… after she…" He puts down the photo and walks towards the piano. I wince. It was him who'd taught me how to play.

"After she died," I supply.

"Yes, after she died. I checked myself into a rehabilitation facility to help with my drinking and gambling addiction," he says. "I've been getting treatment for the last few months, and I've been sober since she left us," he continues, cautiously making his way to the couch.

"Well that's nice," I can't help but say sarcastically. Great for him that he's better now. But what about me?

"Part of the program asks us to go back and make things right."

"Oh, so you're only here because you have to check that box?"

"No, I'm here because I care about you. I love you, kiddo, and I wanted to make things right between us." He says finally taking a seat on the couch opposite from me.

"Now you do? How do you see that working out?"

"I want us to be a family again." I look at him with skepticism brimming in my eyes. Why does he think we'll just go back to being a family?

"A family?"

"Yes, a family. I… There's something else I have to tell you." What else? I nod for him to continue. "Before your mom passed, things weren't going well. It was all my fault, and I realize that now. I drove a wedge between us, and your mom and I… We started having problems. I was addicted to drinking and gambling and every time I lost, I basically lost my shit."

"Okay." I already knew that.

"And, well, one of the biggest fights your mom and I had before she passed was when I told her, I got someone…"

My eyes narrow on him. "You got someone, *what?*"

"I was at a bar watching a fight I had a two thousand dollar bet on, and well, I lost. I was pissed, and there was this…this woman there who had been flirting with me the whole night."

"Oh my god, you cheated on Mom?" I scream, abandoning my seat on the couch.

"Things weren't good at home. We'd stopped sleeping in the same bed. We only shared a bedroom when you visited from college."

"So that makes it better?" I continue to yell, pacing from one end of the room to another.

"No, I know it doesn't," he says, his head hanging in embarrassment. "It only went on for a little while," he adds while standing up.

"You had an affair? Not a one-time thing, but you actually had a fucking affair?"

There was no biting my tongue now.

"Yes, but I ended it, I did. Except, it was too late because the woman…the woman told me she was pregnant." My movements come to a halt.

His words sound like nails scratching a chalkboard. I hear them, but I can't believe they're true.

"You have a sister," he says, and at this, I walk towards the door and leave the house. He calls my name behind me, but I don't stop. I can't stop.

I run. I run like there is someone chasing me because there is. Well not someone, but something—my past. I left California so I never had to cross paths with him. I never wanted to see him again. Not after he left me. Tears fall and my vision blurs, but I don't stop running. I can't stop.

I remember being at mom's funeral. I didn't cry, I didn't speak. I didn't do anything. I couldn't. Because not only had I lost my mom, I had also lost my dad. He wasn't at the funeral, he'd been removed throughout the entire process. I begged and begged for him to come but he didn't. He didn't help make funeral arrangements. He didn't answer any questions. Hadn't said a word to me. Not even a hug. No comfort whatsoever. Never asked how I was doing. I knew he was hurting, but I was too. And he was the parent, not me. He was the only parent I had left.

I had lost one of the most important people in my life and my dad wasn't there to help me through it. Instead, I forced myself to not feel. Even after childhood friends, neighbors, co-workers, and anyone else that knew and loved my mother tried to comfort me. They expressed their deep sadness for my loss. Still, I could feel their confusion, could see their eyes wandering around in search of my father. I was looking for him too.

After we buried her everyone went home. There was nothing else left to do. Natasha, a friend who'd driven from school for the break with me asked if I wanted company, if I needed her. I told her I wanted to be alone.

That was a lie.

I didn't want to be alone.

Moving mechanically, I got out of the car and walked into the house. Inside, the memories of my childhood assaulted me. I felt like I was drowning in an ocean of them. I screamed as loud as I could, hoping to let everything out—hoping to feel something other than the numbness—but it didn't help.

I rushed to my parents' room. I wanted to confront my father and demand answers. I was ready to fight him, too—to scream at him for not being there for me, for not being there for mom. I wrenched the bedroom door open…

No one was there.

Seeing my mother's robe hanging on the headboard broke me. Her things were unmoved, untouched. If it wasn't for the memory of her body in the casket, I'd have expected her home at any minute now.

I moved toward her closet, her favorite place. It's where her collection of boots and scarfs were kept, and right then, I needed to feel closer to her. When I opened the door all I could focus on was the fact that all my father's clothes were missing. Gone. I ran to their bathroom, and nothing of his was there either. I yelled for him, running from room to room, expecting to find him.

Finally, I ran down to the kitchen, where, there on top of the table, was a yellow envelope. I sat down and took a deep breath. I ripped the envelope open, scared of what I would find inside. I found a note and read it.

I'm sorry. I can't do this. Seeing you every day will remind me of her. I'm sorry for hurting our family. I promise I'll get better. I wish I had earlier.

I kept looking to see if there was anything else, and there was. But nothing that made me feel better. My father had left me a court Petition for Emancipation. At the bottom of the document was his signature: Michael Collins.

It took me forever to stop reliving that time in my head. I had worked so hard to push it down. It took me a while to regain control of my life, to feel like a person, to not look at myself in the mirror and hate what I saw, just like my dad did.

I'm still running, and while I thought I was running aimlessly, I find myself slowing down in front of Colton's house. My hair is stuck to my face, the little eyeliner and mascara I'd applied likely smudged. My legs feel weak, my head is pounding, and my heart? Well, my heart is hanging on by a thread. Hanging on because of Colton.

I can hear the booming music and second guess going inside. People will notice. People will see there's something wrong with me. Or maybe they won't. All I know is that I need to see Colton.

I need to be with him.

Inside, I run up the stairs like my life depends on it.

When I reach his room, I open the door, and all the air in my lungs leaves in a rush.

Laying in Colton's bed, under his sheets, is Abbigail. She's naked if the clothes on the floor are any indication. I look around to see if Colton is here, praying he isn't, praying she slept with someone else in his room. I look back at Abbigail, who smirks sinisterly at me and points at the bathroom door. The door is propped open and I can hear the shower running.

I can also see Colton's clothes laying on the floor.

I don't know what to do. I have no idea when everything got so out of hand, but I know I can't stay here. I can't take another person hurting me—not tonight, though maybe it's already too late.

Fresh tears form, falling down my cheeks as I make my way out of the stupid Football House. I should have known better than to come here. Just because someone says they don't need something doesn't mean it's true. Shit, I remember the only thing I needed was to be alone, but that was a lie. Just like Colton lied to me about not having his own needs—needs I couldn't meet, needs Abbigail has always been more than happy to fulfill.

People stare at me as I pass, their eyes full of concern. Not knowing where to go next and not having the strength to keep going, I walk to the side of the Football House, slide down the wall onto the grass and let the tears fall. I cry so much that I don't know if I'll ever be able to cry again.

Why the hell did my father have to return now and destroy the walls I have worked so hard to build? I guess it's not entirely his fault considering Colton had slowly been removing bricks. In the end, the only person to blame is me. Me, and whoever the hell ran a red light and killed my mother.

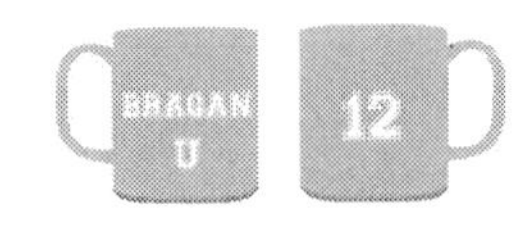

Chapter Twenty-two

COLTON

I finish shaving and wash my face once more. This shower was very needed. After the football game, I went straight to Mia's house. It's funny how a couple of months ago, she wouldn't let me in, and now I spend more time there than here. My time was cut short, though; I needed to help the guys set up for the party—the victory party—because once again, we have made it to the playoffs. We are well positioned to win, and that is a cause for celebration. At least that's what the guys say, but they don't need an excuse.

I dry my face and apply some lotion. I can see myself smiling at the mirror, thinking of how far I've come with Mia. Seriously, the girl has got me moisturizing my face and everything. I give myself another once over in the mirror and walk out of the bathroom. My gaze lands on a bra stacked on top of a pile of clothes on the floor. I turn my head to the right and find Abby laying on my bed.

"What the fuck?"

"Care to join me?" she purrs, devouring me with her eyes. I clutch my towel a little more tightly.

"You need to get out. How many times do I have to say it for you get the point?"

"Oh, come on, you know you want to. For old time's sake." She lowers the sheet enough to reveal her naked breasts.

"You need to get the fuck out of my room right now," I say, keeping my eyes on her face.

She sits up, letting the sheet fall away even more. "Or what?"

"Or I'll make sure you're never welcomed in this house again. Or maybe, maybe I'll tell the administration about how you've been getting an A in biology by screwing the professor."

"You wouldn't," she answers with the deer-caught-in-headlights look.

"You know very well I would. I'll make sure everyone knows exactly who you are and where we stand. Let's see if you'll be head of a sorority then. You'd be lucky if you don't get kicked out of the school."

"Are you threatening to gossip?"

"I'm threatening to tell the truth. Abby, I need you to get out of here." When she doesn't move, I raise my voice, adding, "Now!" Her eyes widen and she sniffs before throwing back the sheets from her naked body. I snatch her clothes from the floor and toss them at her.

"You'll regret this," she says while throwing on her dress.

"I've regretted many things—meeting you, being with you. But this? This is something I know I'll never regret."

"I hate you."

"Good. Hold on to that hate and stay the hell away from me."

She leaves, and I blow out a breath. I know Mia is coming here tonight, and the last thing I need is to remind her of my mistakes, of my history. I start getting dressed, making sure I don't let Abby ruin my mood. The thought of seeing Mia erases the bitterness.

I pull on a shirt then check my phone for any messages from Mia. When I see I don't have any, I make my way downstairs.

Down in the living room, I see the party is in full swing. I still don't know how the hell we fit so many people into this house, but every party seems more packed than the last. I bump fists with Zack then nod at Blake, who are both talking to a few other players.

"Hey, Hunter," Chase calls.

I walk over to where he's standing. "Hey, Boulder. Where's your girl?"

"She's not coming. Said she's not in the mood to party," he shrugs. "How's your girl?"

My girl, yes. Because although we might not be official, I know she is. I can tell by the way she whimpers every time we kiss.

"She's good," I know there's a stupid smirk pasted on my face.

"Good. She looked like she was in bad form when she came in."

My blood runs cold. "What do you mean bad form? When did she come in?" My head starts spinning. I don't know what he means by 'bad form', but the need to know she's okay immediately seizes my body.

"Yeah, she walked in maybe twenty minutes ago, crying. She ran upstairs. I followed her to make sure she was okay, but then I saw her go into your room."

"And then?" I ask, knowing she must have seen Abbigail there.

"I came back down to the party."

"Did you see her come down?"

"No. I thought she was still upsta—"

Before he can finish his sentence, I turn to the rest of the guys. "Did any of you see Mia?"

"Nope," Zack says.

"Nope," Blake adds.

"Is she the hot little thing you've been spending all your free time with?" says a tight end named Connor. I want to punch him in the face, but think better of it. I have priorities, and he isn't one of them right now.

"Yes, did you see her?" I force the words out of my mouth, enunciating every single one carefully.

"Yeah, she came downstairs. Ran out of the house, actually. She was definitely cryi—"

I don't wait for him to finish. I run out of the door as fast as I can.

I hear the distinct sound of Mia's voice, yelling at someone to stop. I run to where I think she may be, and find her trapped between both of Brandon's arms against the side of the house. She looks like she's staring down the barrel of a gun, waiting for the end to come. She's accepting defeat. Her eyes go from him to me, pleading for me to intervene. To do something.

So, I do.

Before I can register anything else, I have Brandon pinned to the brick, using my weight to hold him aloft while my hand wraps around his throat. He's afraid of me. I can tell by the way his eyes beg for mercy. He knows how vicious I can be on the field. Imagine what I could do to him with the right motivation.

His feet hang in the air while I push my shoulder onto his chest. He isn't light, but practice has made me into a beast and I know how to use my weight to my advantage.

"What the fuck do you think you're doing?" I ask in a lethal voice.

"Nothing… I—She… We were just talking," he says, his voice shaking with every word.

"And does she look like she wants to talk to you?" I say emphasizing the word 'talk' as I tighten my hold on his neck. He must think I'm an idiot. Talking was not what he wanted to do with Mia. I feel my heart rate increase, beating so hard it could jump out of my body. My anger rises rapidly, and I know I'm on the verge of losing control.

"Ah, she, I mean, I wanted to make sure she was okay," he responds.

"This is how you make sure someone is okay?" I retort. Every lie he tells makes me want to punch him in the jaw. I exercise as much control as I can. With every question I ask, I think of what could have happened if I hadn't been here. What could have happened to her had I not been looking for her. Each 'what if' adds wood to the already burning fire within me.

"Why does it matter? Back off, Hunter," he says, attempting to sound tough, but his shaking shows otherwise.

"It matters because she's a person, you imbecile, and because she's mine," I growl like a caveman, but it's true. She is mine. She has been since the day she ran into me in class. She would have been mine earlier had I not been too distracted to notice her. She's mine and I'm hers.

Brandon seems to sober up, his eyes widening as he finally grasps how serious I am.

"Hunter, I didn't know she was your girl," he says, trying to downplay the whole situation.

"It shouldn't matter whether she's my girl or not. She said no—that's enough," I say. "I don't ever want to see or hear about you trying to take advantage of a girl again. If I do, you will regret it. Now fuck off. And when it comes to her," I say, pointing to Mia, "Do not look at her, do not touch her, do not think about her, do not approach her. If you see her walk in one direction, you walk the opposite way.

You're lucky I don't kick your ass right now. If I ever see you do this shit again, you won't be so lucky."

I shove him once more against the wall before releasing him. As soon as I do, he runs towards the front of the house.

I'm trying to calm myself down by taking deep breaths, but this is halted when I hear a sob. I turn around to find Mia sitting on the grass. Her knees are drawn toward her chest, her hands covering her mouth to mute her crying. But it's unsuccessful. Tears are running down her beautiful face. She looks so fragile, like someone who is breaking but is desperately trying to keep the pieces together—to keep herself together. I know exactly how she's feeling. I'm always trying to hold shit together, to pick up the pieces, but it never works. Things always manage to break.

I approach her slowly, afraid I might scare her. If she did see Abbigail upstairs, she may be thinking the worst of me right now. Part of me knows this, while the other part of me, the one I have to fight to restrain, wants to run. Wants to run to her. Wants to pick her up from the floor, and hold her in my arms while I provide her with the comfort she needs. The comfort I need too.

I kneel in front of her, and she senses my presence immediately. I wait for her to look up, and when she does, I can tell she's angry. Seeing this, I move to sit next to her instead; I know this will be a serious conversation.

I mirror her posture, embracing my knees as I pull them towards my chest. To anyone else, I probably look awkward as hell, and uncomfortable too. It would be an accurate description, but it's where I need to be.

She looks away from me, not saying a word.

Still, I'm not going to leave her alone—not unless she asks me to, and even then, I'm not sure how far I'd go. I am willing to be her shoulder to cry on, or her punching bag to lash out at. I'm willing to be whatever she needs me to be.

When she stops crying, she tries to compose herself. I look in her direction to see her shake her head. I lift my eyebrows questioningly. After a few awkward minutes, she finally makes eye contact and the disappointment I see in her eyes breaks me.

MIA

"Hey, are you okay?" he asks.

"I'm fine. I'm not a damsel in distress. I don't need you saving me," I bite back. Screw him and his kindness. It's all an act.

"That's not what it looked like when I got here," he says, visibly irritated.

Well, screw him.

"I was handling it." And I was about to handle him, too.

"Really, how? By crying?"

"I had it under control. I was just about to do something about it." And I was. I was just caught off guard. I saw the guy approach, and I immediately got up, but before I could move away, he caged me in. For a second, I contemplated doing nothing, just letting it happen. Why resist when people hurt you anyway? It appears that regardless of how much I try to not let people continue to destroy me, they do. So, this time it was going to be my choice.

Before I caved into that feeling, the rational part of my brain knew that this wasn't me. I was just about to stop him, but then Colton came up behind him.

"That certainly looked like it was under control," he states. Funny that he seems to care so much about what happens to me.

"Just like you had Abby under control upstairs?" I respond, daring him to contradict me.

"That wasn't what—"

"That wasn't what I thought? Is that what you were going to say?"

"Mia."

"Are you going to tell me I didn't see Abbigail upstairs, in your bed, naked?"

"Yes, but—"

"Yeah, but nothing. I saw what I saw, Colton."

"Yes, but you don't understand—"

"I do understand. I am nothing to you. I knew it from the beginning. I knew you weren't boyfriend material. I knew you would play with my heart like you play with every other girl's, like it's a game. But honestly, this isn't your fault. It's mine. But you know what? I don't care anymore."

"Those tears tell me otherwise. Clearly, I mean something to you."

"You meant something to me, but that was my mistake."

"No, it wasn't, Mia."

I stand up, turn around and start walking away when I feel a cold hand grab my arm.

"What do you want?" I demand.

"You."

"How poetic. You want her, too. And every other girl."

"No, Mia. If it hasn't been clear to you from the last few months we've spent together, I want you. I *only* want you."

"Somehow I don't believe you." Sarcasm drips from my words. This isn't a telenovela. This isn't a happily ever after romance story where those words would sweep me off my feet.

"Mia—"

I pull my arm away and walk in the direction of my apartment.

"You can't walk away from this," he says desperately.

I whirl around to face him. "Like you've faced all your demons? Please. Cut the bull."

"Just wait. You can't leave."

"Watch me."

He appears at my side, matching my every stride. "No. You can't walk away from an argument, from a fight. You have to stay and fix it."

"Not all things can be fixed, and not all things are meant to be fixed. You should know," That's the last thing I say before walking away, once again leaving it all behind.

I walk through the door just as Kiya is about to walk out to head to the party. Colton's party. The party we were both supposed to go to, but one look at my face makes her cancel her plans.

"What's wrong?" Kiya asks, but I don't really know how to answer.

I go with the easier version. "A lot."

"Come here," Kiya pulls me into a bear hug. I know it's supposed to make me feel better, but all it does is open the dam, and the tears start to fall again. She lets go of me, drops her purse, shakes off her heels and grabs my arm, pulling me towards the kitchen.

"Let's talk about it over spiked Oreo shakes," she says. Because my roommate knows that nothing else will get me to talk.

I sit at the kitchen table, waiting for Kiya to finish her magic drink. Finally, she places a glass in my hand while guiding me to the living room. When she sits on the couch, I follow. She turns on the TV, and I am thankful for every minute she gives me to pull myself together. At this moment, I am thankful I still have her in my life.

"You ready?"

"As I'll ever be."

"So, what happened?"

"My dad stopped by the house today. My dad, who after my mom was killed on her way to pick up his drunk ass from a bar, didn't go to her funeral. Who, after leaving me, decided to finally show up," I yell. I feel myself getting angrier by the second, each statement bringing back a new memory.

"Oh, my God. No wonder you've never mentioned him. I'm so sorry, Mia. What did he want?"

"He wanted to explain, a second chance. A do-over!" I state.

"And?"

"I'm not really about giving second chances to people who don't deserve them. I mean, why open myself to getting hurt twice by the same person? It doesn't make any sense." I know that as I say this to my roommate, I'm really talking to myself too.

No second chances for people who don't deserve them.

"So, what did you do?"

"When I opened the door and saw his face, I didn't know what to do. I was angry, but…for a brief second, I was also glad to see him–the fact he was alive and looked like a decent human being. My father took my silence as permission to speak and asked for forgiveness. He said he'd gone to rehab, that he's been sober since the day Mom died."

"That's good."

"And, he also said there's someone else in his life."

"Oh, shit. Really?"

"Yeah, and that broke me. Mom hasn't been dead for long, and while he couldn't be there for me, he has been there for his other daughter. The one he wants me to meet."

"Oh, M, I know that probably hurt. But you might want to try to forgive him. He is your dad, after all."

"He sure as hell forgot to act like it when I needed him the most. No need to start now."

"You might want to give him a chance though? That way you won't regret it."

"Anyway," I say moving the conversation along. "I didn't know what else to do, so I ran away from my own house."

"No wonder you looked like a wet raccoon when you came in the house." My roommate tries to lighten the mood with a joke. I don't think she's joking though.

"I ran over to Colton's house."

"Of course you did. You guys are inseparable. I don't know where you end and he begins anymore. And I really don't know how you stop yourself from sleeping with him. If you weren't my friend, I would have my hands all over that."

Bracing myself, I push through. "I'm sure I'll have no problem with that," I answer. My words are biting.

"Is everything okay?"

"I think you already know it's not."

"Did something happen with Colton, too?"

"I ran to his house, and because I'm an idiot, I just let myself in his room and found Abbigail in his bed. Naked."

Kiya's mouth hangs open. "No shit. What the… You're kidding, right?" I wish I was.

"I guess knowing he wouldn't be able to get any from me made him get it from somewhere else."

"Mia. I'm shocked, truly." She takes my free hand and squeezes it. "I'm so sorry. I never saw him as the type to do the whole celibate thing. I mean for the last few years, he's had his pick of women and rarely turned them down, if the rumors were any indication, but he seems different with you—not just when he's around you, but overall. Blake tells me about it all the time. Shoot, watching the two of you was making me believe in fairytales. True love and shit."

"Well, don't believe in it. Clearly, it's not real."

"What did he say?" she asks, then adds, "Sorry, if you don't want to talk about it, you don't have to."

"No, it's fine. I need to get it off my chest. He was in the shower when I came in, so I left. He found me outside, said he could 'explain'." I put the word "explain" in quotation marks because how the hell could you explain sleeping with someone else?

'I'm sorry, my dick made me do it.'

Yeah, right.

"Are you sure? I mean, you didn't actually catch him sleeping with her. And Abbigail is a bitch."

"His clothes were on the floor. I mean, I can be naïve, but the evidence was there. Trust me, I wish it wasn't true, but it is."

"I don't know what to say."

"You don't have to say anything. It's okay."

"It's *not* okay."

I shrug. "It will be," I say to her, and myself. I've been through worse and managed to come out on the other end. This will be no different.

"I love you," my roommate says, hugging me again.

"I love you, too." And I do. Kiya is like the sister I never had.

"Okay, okay. Enough with the sappiness. We'll cry tonight, but start over tomorrow. Deal?"

"Deal, but please make more of this magical drink," I say, lifting my glass in the air.

"Oh, that's not magic. That's Godiva chocolate liqueur."

"Whatever it is, it tastes like magic. Give me more. I'm in pain." I laugh, handing her the glass. Things may be crappy right now, but I have Kiya, and I know she'll be here for me.

"You're a pain." My roommate gets up off the couch and heads to the kitchen.

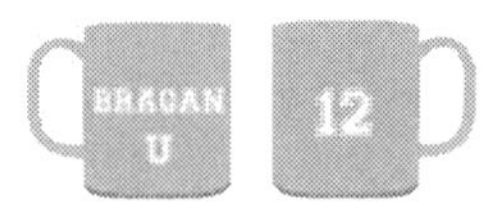

Chapter Twenty-three

COLTON

It's been a long ass month since I last talked to Mia. She's been ignoring me, refusing to talk to me, to straighten things out. I can't believe how much I miss her.

I miss everything about her, her laugh, her sass, her kisses. I miss how genuine she is, and how gorgeous she is without even realizing it. Even working on this damn assignment with her made it more tolerable. She made everything better, she made me better, and my history fucked that up.

I haven't been able to type more than three words on the part she assigned to me—the same part I had when we worked on the outline. I almost don't want to do it, maybe then she'll talk to me. I'll take her anger over her silence any day.

Even this room feels different without her here. I'm sitting at my desk. My computer is on, but there's nothing else I can think of but her.

I can't believe Abbigail did this—ruined everything.

Why would Mia even think I was capable of doing this shit? I told her what my mom is doing. I told her I despise cheaters, yet she thinks I would do the same?

I thought Mia understood me, but apparently, she doesn't.

My phone rings, interrupting my thoughts. Hope grows within me. Maybe she misses me enough to reach out and finally let me explain.

But that hope is soon extinguished when I see it's my dad calling.

"Hey, Dad," I say, flatly.

"Hey, son, how are you?" That's the fifty-million-dollar question everyone and their mothers have been asking me lately. I guess it's pretty obvious that I feel like shit because all the guys have been asking. Even Kaitlyn and Nick stopped by to make sure I was doing okay. I shut them out too. There's only one person that could make me feel remotely better, and sadly, she's the reason I feel like shit.

"I'm doing…" I stop there because honestly, I don't know.

"Last time you were here…" he starts.

Oh, here we go.

"You didn't seem like you were okay. I know there's something going on between you and your mom."

"Yeah," I answer. I shouldn't fault my dad for working hard every day. I know he's obsessed with work because he sees it as a way to provide for us, but I see it as the one thing that's prevented him from realizing what I've now known for a very long time.

"We should talk about whatever it is that's bothering you, son."

"We don't need to."

"We do. I feel like we never see you around the house anymore, and when we do, it's like you don't want to be here, or you and your mom get into a fight."

"I was just tired, Dad."

"I raised you myself and I can tell when something is bothering you, Colt. Whatever it is, you can tell me."

Sure, I can.

"You can."

I said that out loud. "Dad—"

"Son, you used to look up to me at one point. I don't know what I've done to change that, but I want you to know I love you. I care about you, and I need to know what's going on."

"Okay, fine," I state because I'm sick and tired of carrying around someone else's weight. I shouldn't have to be the one to figure this out. Kaitlyn and Nick should know too—it's been too long. If shit goes south, I'll have their back. I always do. It can be all of us against them.

"Great. Let's meet at the diner we used to go to for dinner every Sunday. What was it called again?"

"West Side Diner," I respond, the thought of Mia sitting at my favorite booth immediately coming to mind.

"Okay, I can meet you there. What's your schedule look like for tomorrow?"

I glance at the calendar that sits on my desk. Class, meetings, and practice.

"I can meet you there at six."

"Sounds good."

I pause for a beat, licking my lips. "Could you do me a favor?"

"Yes, son, always."

"Don't tell Mom." I don't want her to see this coming.

"I—Okay," he says. We say our goodbyes and hang up.

Mia was right about one thing. I was acting like a coward by not facing my own problems, but that changes tomorrow. First my father, then my girl.

I pull into the diner like I have many times before. I thought about whether I should actually go through with this, but decided it was time. It's unfair to my father and my siblings to be completely unaware. They'll probably hate me for keeping it to myself for so long, but I felt like I had no choice. But Mia's taught me that everyone has a choice. And today, I'm choosing to face this shit head on.

I park in my usual spot and jump out of the car. Like taking off a bandage, the quicker I do this, the less it'll hurt. Who am I kidding? It'll hurt still. It'll wreak havoc in our family, but maybe that's what we need so we can start over.

I go through the front door, recognizing some of the waitresses on today.

"Table for two in Karla's section please," I tell the hostess.

"I'm sorry, but Karla isn't on today. Would you still like to be seated?" she asks.

"Sure."

"Can I tell your waitress to put in an order for you while you wait?" she asks me.

"A Jack and Coke, please." I need more than one drink to help me get through this conversation tonight but, at least, it's a start.

This is harder than I thought it would be and I haven't even started yet.

A few minutes later, my father walks through the door. He's wearing a business suit under a cashmere coat. Likely, he's just come from the office. I see his eyes roam around the room until he spots me. As he walks to me, I brace myself for the discussion we're about to have because nothing will be the same after this.

"Hey, Colt," my dad says as he slides into the booth.

"Hi, Dad," I tell him as the waitress brings over my drink and places it on the table.

"Ah, I think I'm going to be needing one of those too," my dad says, pointing at my glass.

"You will," I reply. The waitress nods and turns away.

We both watch her leave, both trying to prolong the inevitable.

"What's going on with you and your mom, son?" my father says as soon as his drink is set in front of him. He doesn't waste any time, wants to get right into it. I guess that's a quality I get from him.

Chapter Twenty-Four

MIA

It's been a month since I've spoken to Colton. A month since I walked into his room and found Abby sprawled on his bed. A month of not knowing if he's called or texted because he's still blocked. A month of changing my routine so I can avoid running into him. I know if I give him a chance to talk to me, I'll give in. Because although I look like I'm over it, although I think I'm strong, I'm not. I miss him so much I cry myself to sleep every night, my pillow the only one to know my secret.

I've thought about whether he could be telling the truth when he told me he didn't sleep with her. I've run scenario upon scenario of how it would play out in his benefit but none of them result in a logical explanation. It's just me trying to find a way to still be with him. Because, although I don't know how it happened, I'm in love with him. I fell in love without even realizing it. He took over my heart, piece by piece. The only pieces I have left crave to be back with him.

But I can't go back.

Knowing he slept with her keeps me from running back to him. I can't let myself go there again. I can't open myself up to be hurt, and so I'll just go on with my life as if he was never a part of it.

I know I'm broken, but I deserve more.

I walk into class with minutes to spare, finding my seat at the front of the room. I breathe a sigh of relief knowing that even though I no longer get here fifteen minutes early, I can still find my old seat empty. At least something has remained consistent.

The class is already full, and I face forward, waiting for the professor to start. Out of the corner of my eye, I see Colton walk in. He looks as gorgeous as ever, but I force myself to stop watching. I wait for him to head to his normal seat, but he starts walking in my direction instead.

"Excuse me," he says as he stands in front of the girl to my right.

"Yes?" she says flirtatiously, and I can't help but feel jealous. I have no right to though, because he isn't mine. He never really was.

"Do you mind if we switch seats? I'm having a little trouble seeing from the back."

My breath hitches.

"Of course!" the girl says excitedly. I bet she's feeling rather special that he talked to her.

"Thanks," he says and drops his things next to mine.

I am so aware of him that it feels as if the air is crackling with tension.

"You can't keep doing this," he whispers to me as the professor starts to talk about citations. I ignore him.

"I need to talk to you," Colton insists.

"We're in class," I state.

"I don't give a fuck."

"Mr. Hunter, Ms. Collins, would you like a second to finish your conversation?"

I feel the class' attention move from the professor to us. "No, all set," I respond, embarrassed we were called out.

"You're going to have to talk to me," Colton says after Clift moves on. As much as it hurts me, I keep my eyes on the board, pretending to take notes on whatever the professor is saying, pretending like my heart isn't breaking.

Colton continues to sit next to me in every class we have together. Every time I switch my seat, in the hopes that he'll stop trying to explain because I don't want to hear it. Today, I decided to sit in the back row, hoping that his excuse of not being able to see won't work and he'd stop following me.

"Talk to me," he says as he takes the seat next to me.

"There's not much to talk about."

"Bullshit. I didn't sleep with her. You know I would never want to."

"How do I know that? How do I know you haven't slept with the whole female population?" I spit back.

"I haven't. Just let me explain."

"No."

"Why not?"

Because I might believe you. "Because it's better this way."

"Better for who?" he asks, his tone accusatory.

"Better for both of us. I get to focus on school and…and you get to focus on your family, maybe get a girlfriend that's in your league so you don't cheat on her."

"What the *fuck* does that mean?"

"Which part?"

"The girlfriend on my level part," he deadpans, and I blush.

"You're the QB of one of the best college teams. You are literally from a different world than me. I think you'd do better with someone you can parade around without shame."

"Where is this coming from?" he says, not denying he'd be better off with someone like him.

"It just makes sense. The popular guy and shy nerdy girl never work out." This isn't the conversation I want to have, but if it gets him to stop, then I have to.

"Do you think I can't parade you around?" he asks.

"I think you'd do better with parading someone around who will make you look better and fulfill your needs," I scoff.

"Mia, you don't just make me look better, you *make* me better."

I don't respond.

"Ms. Collins and Mr. Hunter, if you think I can't see that the two of you are having your own conversation, you are clearly mistaken. Care to share with the rest of us what's so important it can't wait until class ends?" the professor asks, and all eyes turn to us.

"Nothing," I respond, sliding down in the chair to hide myself from the curious stares.

"Actually, I'd love to," Colton says, and my eyes connect with his immediately, wondering what he's going to do.

"Please, proceed," the professor says, challenging Colton.

"Well, I was just telling Ms. Collins that I am in love with her. That no other girl could ever come close to how I feel about her. And it would be an honor to hold her hand and have the world know that she's mine and I'm hers."

In love?

Shocked gasps reverberate through the classroom.

"I wanted to know if she would like to formally be mine," he says, taking his seat once more.

Professor Clift laughs and looks at me. "So, Ms. Collins, I'm sure everyone is interested in knowing what your answer is. This is the first time I've heard of Mr. Hunter begging for something. You must be very special."

I can't believe the professor isn't pissed about the interruption. I'm even more surprised he's encouraging it.

I look around the room, seeing the expressions of my classmates. Many looked amused, some are jealous, and others are just straight up shocked. I find Abbigail watching me with a snarl and I immediately wonder if her plan was to make me believe he'd been with her.

I look at Colton as he stares back at me. Waiting for me to answer him. His eyes dare me to challenge his words, to deny him.

"I…" I start.

"Yes?" he asks, looking at me hopefully.

I can feel myself caving, his every word being exactly what I need. Before I give in, I grab my things and walk out of the class.

I've not even taken three steps out of the building when Colton catches up to me, pulling me to a stop. I glare at him.

"You've said your piece. Now you will listen to mine," he says.

I hate being told what to do with a passion, but my feet stay planted on the ground, despite my head yelling at me to leave. I don't really need this drama in my life, but my heart, the one that's been pulling me in the opposite direction more and more each day, tells me to stay and hear him out. And like every single cliché, I do. I stop and turn to face him with tears pooling in my eyes.

"Listen, I didn't know Abby was there."

"You figured she'd leave immediately after you had sex with her?"

"No, not that. We…I… I didn't sleep with her. I haven't slept with her for months. We stopped before I met you."

If he expects me to believe this, he must be out of his damn mind. I dry the tears from my face because he's not worth it.

He continues, not letting me interrupt. "I don't know if you've noticed, but you're the only girl I have eyes for."

He takes hold of my hand, stopping me from walking away. I want to pull away, but even now, even here, his touch calms me and makes me forget the storm that has hit my life.

"You can ask all the guys if you want. Listen, Abbigail is jealous of you. She's jealous because you made me do what she never had the ability to. You made me want to be faithful, to be better, to be yours and only yours. I swear to you, baby, I didn't know she was in my room.

"The moment I got home from seeing you, I helped the guys set up for the party. Then I ran upstairs to shower. I must have forgotten to lock the door. I walked out of the bathroom and there she was. I threw her clothes at her, kicked her out and told her to leave me alone."

The words are flying out of his mouth like he's afraid I won't let him finish.

"I went downstairs, and the guys told me you'd been upstairs, but ran out crying. And fuck, if that didn't hurt. The thought of losing you hurt more than I thought it would. You own me, Mia. You own every part of me, and without you, I can't breathe.

"Please, believe me. You make me better. I've never been as open with someone as I have with you. I've never had someone tell me they were going to be there for me in every way. You offered to talk to me whenever I needed someone to talk to. Whether it was late at night, or early in the morning. You made it easy for me to trust you. And right now, baby, more than ever, I need you to trust me. I need you to believe me."

I want to tell him I believe him. I do. But I don't know if it's because I truly do or because my heart wants me to. We are so different that even if, and that's a big if, he didn't sleep with her, I know I can't give him what he wants. There are so many others that could. Even if he is telling the truth, this—the two of us—we aren't going to make it. So, I let my mind take control instead of my heart.

"I don't," I say softly and walk away.

Chapter Twenty-five

MIA

"Hey, Mia! Stop," I hear a girl say from behind me as I walk to class two days later. I keep walking. Mia is a common name.

"Hello? Can you please stop walking so fast," the girl says again, and I know she's talking to me. I turn on my heel and see Kaitlyn coming towards me. The wind causing her hair to fly all over her face, but still looking as gorgeous as ever. I guess it runs in the family.

"I didn't think you knew my name," I say as she steps up to me. She's breathing like she's just run a marathon.

"I deserve that," she says, looking at her feet.

"It's okay. Most people don't know who I am."

"I just wanted to say something."

I look at her impatiently. "Could you spit it out? I have to go," I say, looking behind her to see if her brother is somewhere in sight.

"Looking for Colton?" she asks, following my eyes.

"Looking to avoid him," I say honestly.

"He didn't sleep with her."

I roll my eyes. "Of course he didn't," I respond sarcastically.

"Seriously, he didn't."

"Why should I believe you? You're his sister." Definitely an unreliable source.

"You should believe me because I *am* his sister, because I know him better than anyone else except maybe Nick."

Apparently not well enough to notice he's been beating himself up over a family secret he's had to keep.

"And," she adds, noticing I'm not buying what she's selling. "I know Abbigail. I've been living in the same house as her for the last two years," she says disgustedly, like living with Abbigail is the worst thing she's ever had to do. I don't disagree.

"You guys are like best friends," I remind her.

"Oh, God, no. She's a bitch."

"So, why do you hang out with her?"

Why am I even entertaining this conversation? I need to go to class then go home where I can have the special Kiya Oreo shake while I mope.

"Because being cool with her was the only way I could be a part of DM."

"I don't know if being in a sorority is worth dealing with her."

"Ain't that the truth," she mutters. "Anyway, I wanted to tell you that they didn't sleep together. Abbigail lied. She told the girls last night that she'd let herself into Colton's room that night. She said she was going to seduce him and try to get him to give into her charms, but you walked in and saw her. She was laughing about how her plan couldn't have been any better, and now that you were out of the picture, she was going to try and get back into it."

I can't believe the words that are coming out of her mouth. Scratch that, I can. "Are you saying Colton didn't sleep with her that night?"

"They had a thing before, but he broke it off. He didn't want her, and he doesn't want her now. Abbigail knew that and felt threatened." She shrugged. "So, I wanted you to know that the way

I see my brother speak of you, the way the guys taunt him about you and he responds, I know he has feelings for you. Real feelings. He's usually closed off, but right now we can all tell he's hurting."

"Oh." I don't know what to say.

"Don't give up on him, not yet."

"I…" What am I supposed to do?

"And Mia, thanks for having my back that night at Eclipse."

"No problem," I say, finally finding words to respond.

"Sorry it took me so long to have yours," she says, walking away.

I take a seat in the front of the classroom, waiting for class to begin and mulling over everything that Kaitlyn told me a few minutes ago. I'm waiting for Colton to sit next to me again when he walks in, but he doesn't. I see him walk toward the back of the class, and force myself to not look in his direction.

After class, Colton stops me outside the room, tugging me into a quiet corner.

"I need you to understand that I want nothing to do with Abbigail, or any other girl in this school." I look down at my shoes, and he lifts my chin to meet his eyes, the ones that have resonated with me since the day I met him. The ones that hold so much promise, pain, power, and in this very moment, hope.

"From the first day I met you, I knew you were different, and I like who I am when I'm with you. I love you and only you, and I think you love me too. I just needed you to know because every kiss we've shared made me feel like you were mine." He wipes away the tear I hadn't realized had fallen. "You own me. I'm yours, and only yours. Are you mine, Mia? Could you be mine? Because every time I say your name, it feels like you are."

"I…" I don't know how to answer because I am his. "I trust you, I know you. And yes, I love you. I know you didn't sleep with her, and I'm sorry I didn't believe you."

His face lights up with a smile. He lifts me up, holding me tightly against his chest.

"You know, every time I say your name, I smile because it means 'mine', and that's all I've ever wanted you to be."

"You're corny," I joke, my heart soaring, my worries forgotten.

"But you love me. You just said that," he tells me with a smile.

"Didn't peg you as the lovey-dovey type."

He taps the tip of my nose with his index finger. "I didn't peg myself as the lovey-dovey type either, but you bring it out in me."

"So, does that mean we're boyfriend and girlfriend now?" I ask, a little embarrassed. Maybe he doesn't want to label it, but labels work for me. They help me figure out what the expectations are.

"Yes, we're boyfriend and girlfriend now," he answers, his lips crashing down on mine. When I'm with Colton, all I feel is comfort, love, care, and everything that's good in life. He lifts me up like I am weightless as he continues to devour me. No words are exchanged between us. None are necessary. The kiss says it all.

COLTON

"My dad came back," Mia says while we're laying in my bed the next day.

I sit up and lean against the headboard. "What do you mean he came back? When?"

"Well, I was on my way to your house the night of the party when my dad showed up."

"What did he want?"

I listen in shocked silence as she recounts their conversation. "And then I ran to your place as fast as I could."

"Why didn't you say something last night?" I ask, playing with her hair as she lays on my chest. I still can't believe we're together. Last night, we came back to the house, stripped the sheets off the bed and tossed them. Then we laid down and talked—talked about when we started having feelings for each other, and about every memory we've made.

"That night started off real shitty, but it ended well. I didn't want to ruin it."

"Babe, you were there for me when I needed you the most. You were the one who told me I needed to speak up and confront my parents. Sharing your problems with me won't ruin anything; it'll just strengthen us."

"Babe? Is that my official pet name?"

"One of many," I say. "What did your dad want?"

She's quiet for a moment. "He wanted to start over—a second chance. He also wanted me to meet my new sister."

"Your new what? What did you say?"

"Sister. It's a long story but the short version is he was with another woman before my mom passed and the rest is history. Honestly, I wasn't really feeling up to giving him a second chance, but now that I think about it, I think I'll try. Better to try than regret it, right?" she asks, looking for confirmation in my eyes.

"If you'll spend your life wondering what a relationship with your father and new sister would be like, then yeah, I think you should give it a try."

"He says he's changed."

"People do."

"I hope so," she says, and I know she's referring not just to her father, but to me, too.

"Trust me."

"Always. Sorry I didn't before."

"You don't have to apologize. I made a rep for myself. I'm the only one at fault. I'm just glad you gave me a chance."

"Well, your sister helped."

"She did?" I ask, wondering what the hell my sister had done.

"Yeah. She said something about you pining over me?"

"She exaggerates," I say jokingly. My sister was right, though. I think I might have bought a few pints of ice cream, too.

"How's your family?" she hesitantly asks, running her fingers down my chest.

"I took your advice," I respond.

She lifts her head slightly, searching my eyes. "What advice?"

"I came clean."

"You did what?" she says, shooting upright.

"I told dad everything."

"And?" she asks, worry clear in her eyes.

"He said he would handle it." And he did.

"How?"

"Adaline's threat was unfounded. He had a paternity test done when Kaitlyn and Nick were born because he suspected even back then that my mother was cheating on him. My brother and sister are his."

"Are you doing okay?"

"I'm fine."

"And your mom?"

"What about her?"

"Did she say something to defend herself?"

"Dad filed for a divorce. He's being generous by giving her enough money to sustain her lifestyle, though he didn't have to since her infidelity was a condition of the prenup."

"Where is she now?"

I sigh deeply. "Don't really know. Don't really care, to be honest. I'm just glad it's over with."

"Me too," she says, and lowers her mouth to mine. I take control of the kiss, causing her to whimper. I silently ask for more, and she gives it to me, and with her acquiescence, I get the same feeling I've had from the first time my lips touched hers—confirmation that she was made for me.

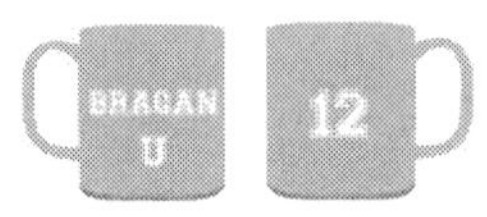

Chapter Twenty-six

MIA

"M, hurry up!" Kiya yells. "We're going to miss the beginning of the game!"

"I'm coming, I'm coming. Just breathe!"

"Don't tell me to breathe," she replies indignantly. "And get out of the bathroom already."

I finish off the last curl, turn off the wand and exit our hotel room bathroom.

"Okay, I'm ready. What do you think?" I spin around so she gets a good look at what I'm wearing: jeans, boots and a number 12 jersey, which I'm wearing because I love Tom Brady and the National Championship is at Gillette Stadium. But also, because it happens to be Colton's number.

Kiya whistles. "Colton's going to lose his shit! He won't be able to concentrate on the game."

"No, he won't." I giggle, although the shock factor is exactly what I'm going for.

"He's a caveman. You wearing his jersey is letting him know you belong to him. You're adding wood to the already burning fire!"

"We belong to each other," I correct her. "It's the least I can do.

This is my first game."

"And his last for the year, so can we hustle and get there on time? Why did you skip all the games, by the way?" she adds.

"Because I wasn't really into college football."

She lifts her eyebrows suggestively. "I guess you have an interest now."

"You're one to talk, Mrs. Miller," I say, pointing at her jersey, which has Blake's last name on the back.

She winks. "Not Mrs. Miller yet."

"Things are getting serious between you two?"

"If they weren't, I wouldn't be wearing his name." She stares at me pointedly, like I'm in exactly the same boat.

And I am.

Ever since our fight and subsequent makeup, Colton and I have been closer than ever, spending time together whenever we can–movie nights, cuddling, make-out sessions. Oh, the make out sessions! Waking up next to him every morning is something I can definitely get used to.

Our relationship has pissed off more people than it should have. Ever since we walked into class hand-in-hand, the rumor mill has run hot and fast. By the time we were out of class, half the school knew we were dating. Things have quieted down a little now, especially with the excitement over the upcoming game. The haters still hate, but I have my man and that's all that matters.

Kiya and I walk the short distance from the hotel to Gillette Stadium and it feels like our whole school has come out to support the team. Students walk in groups of various sizes, all heading in the direction of the stadium, all buzzing with barely-contained energy. I don't blame them. The hype for this game started when the team made it to the National Championship. Luckily, the Championship game is being played in a stadium a couple of hours away from the school, which would explain why I see more blue and white than the purple and white of the other team.

As we walk, everyone sings the fight song, some with their faces painted, some wearing jerseys with Colton's number on the back, and for a moment, I feel like just another face in the crowd. That is until I remember what he told me last night, and again this morning.

"I've already won because I have you, Mia."

Kiya and I get lost in the excitement, both of us a little more passionate than the rest because while they'll be watching and cheering for the team, Kiya and I will be cheering for our boyfriends.

We make it to the stadium just in the nick of time. Finding our way to the bleachers, we follow the signs to our seats at the fifty-yard line, giving us an amazing view of the whole field. I stand there, in awe of how great our seats are and how vast the stadium is. Colton's favorite team, and mine, play here. I glance around and spot a few of the guys and girls from class, and I remember Colton saying that while we didn't have box seats, the players managed to get tickets for their family and friends around the same section.

Beside me, a man says, "I'm glad you made it. You must be Mia." I stare at him, momentarily speechless. He must be Colton's father if the height, eyes, and startling resemblance are any indication.

"How did you know?"

"Oh, you know—" he shrugs, "You might not be the only one wearing his jersey, but you're the one who will be sitting next to me. Plus, Colton's description of you is spot on."

I blush at his comment. "Yes, sir, I am. You must be Mr. Hunter."

"William. It's a pleasure to finally meet you," he says, and I extend my arm ready to shake his hand. He looks down at it and smiles. "From the many times I've heard Colton, Nick, and

Kaitlyn talk about you, it's clear you're part of the family now. So, put that hand away and give me a proper hug." He pulls me in for an embrace, and it's very fatherly—comforting.

I introduce Kiya to him and we all take our seats.

We make small talk, chatting about football, college, and the typical 'getting to know you' questions. As we talk, I see that a lot of Colton's qualities come from his dad, including his smile, which gives me a glimpse of an older version of Colton. I can tell old age will be good to him.

I know it must have been hard for William to deal with his wife's infidelity, but having her out of the picture has only improved his relationship with his kids. He's been spending more time with them and it seems that this debacle was exactly the kind of wake-up call he needed to appreciate the time he has with them.

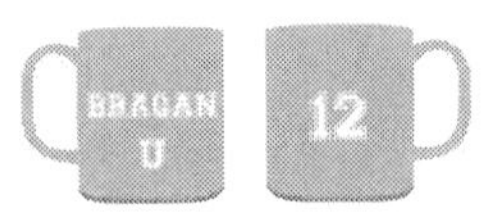

Chapter Twenty-seven

MIA

I've been trying to remain calm, to make a good impression since Colton's father is sitting next to me, but I gave up after the first quarter. Seeing the opposing team go right through our offensive line and sack Colton five times has me fired up. I'm confident I will not have a voice tomorrow with all the yelling I'm doing, but that doesn't stop me from doing it.

To my surprise, after the second quarter, I'm joined by Kiya and Colton's father in the sideline coaching and refereeing, each of us yelling at the top of our lungs.

At halftime, we're still down twenty-one points. I head inside, grab some refreshments for all of us, and pray that whatever 'talk' the coach is having with the team will transform them into better players. They're not a bad team, but their opponents are tough and have been kicking them around the field, exploiting their weaknesses.

The third quarter starts the same way, and I can feel the energy that once consumed the stadium decline. Massively. Everyone's already given up hope, but a touchdown in the last few minutes of the third quarter restores a little bit of faith.

By the fourth quarter, our team has made an incredible comeback. The score is 28-21, and while we've made it this far, we're still down by seven points with only three minutes on the clock. The opposing team's offense takes the field, and unless we get a turnover, it's unlikely we'll get the chance to score again.

The quarterback on the opposing team throws a pass down the middle to one of their receivers, but it is intercepted by number thirty-two. Next to me, Kiya jumps from her seat and cheers for Blake as he runs the ball back toward the end zone. He gets tackled at the other team's twenty-yard line, and while a touchdown would have been great, this play was an answer to my prayers; the interception has put us back in the game.

The two-minute warning is called. The ball is snapped to Colton. He passes it to Ian, who then runs it into the end zone.

"Touchdown!" the announcer screams, and the crowd goes wild, jumping up and cheering. Our chances of winning are at an all-time high.

The score is 27-28 with only fifteen seconds left on the playing clock. The kicker, Jesse, takes the field along with the other players. All he has to do is kick the ball right through the goal posts and get us that game-tying extra point. Hopefully, we can take the game into overtime from there.

The players get into position and the ball is snapped to the holder. Jesse prepares himself for the kick, but instead of the holder setting the football in place, he fakes it and runs it to the left side of the field. The ball is passed to Nick, who runs it the final few yards into the end zone. The two-point conversion is ours, giving us our first lead in the game.

The crowd screams in excitement and start streaming toward the field when the opposing team's Hail Mary, thrown as the clock ran out, is shut down by Chase.

Our team has won.

We won!

Colton's dad beams as he cheers in support of his sons. Kiya and I are right there with him, both overcome with pride for what they've done—the incredible game our boyfriends have played.

COLTON

"Holy shit, man! We did it!" Zack yells as we all run to the end zone to meet Nick. The fans have left their seats and are running towards us at full speed. It's a pool of white and blue. I make it to where the rest of the guys are and pat Nick on the shoulder. These men here did all it took. They played their hearts out, never giving up. I could not be prouder to have played this game with them.

I feel like I'm on top of the world. The buzzing, the screaming fans, the final score on the board. Shit, even the smell of the field makes me feel alive. But I can tell something is missing… No, not something. Someone.

I look at the seat where I know my girl is, and I start walking to her. A few people pat me on the back. Some ask me to sign merchandise or parts of their body. Some even ask to take a picture. Normally, I'd probably grunt and keep moving, but I'm on a high and nothing can ruin my mood.

Suddenly, a female reporter shoves a microphone in my face. "Colton, you made an incredible comeback!"

"Our team did," I correct.

"They looked ready to throw in the towel at the end of the first half. What did you tell them to get them back in the game?" she presses.

"I just told them it's not over until the clock runs out," I respond. My eyes are focused behind her to where I know Mia is.

"How do you plan on celebrating this victory?"

I look back at the reporter. "With my team and with my family."

"Do you think you'll go pro?"

I avoid her question, my attention once again on getting to Mia. "I'm just extremely lucky to have the opportunity to play right now."

"I can see you're looking for someone in the crowd. Do you have someone special you played for?" the reporter asks, trying to keep up with me as I walk.

"I played for my girl," I say, a dorky-ass smile on my face. I can't help it. I will claim her as mine whenever I can. Shit, calling her mine is something I've waited a long time to do, and the fact that I can do it freely now makes me the luckiest bastard alive.

I pick up the pace, leaving the reporter and her questions behind. I find myself jogging, desperate to get to her. There is no one else I'd rather share this moment with. I make it to the fifty-yard line and find her standing with her back to me talking to my dad and Kiya. It gives me the chance to see my last name printed on her back. I hop over the small wall that separates us.

"One day, my last name won't just be on the back of your shirt," I say, wrapping my arms around her waist and pulling her in close.

She turns around and smiles. "Oh y eah?" Her eyes take in my uniform and I can tell she likes what she sees. She runs her fingers over my chest, lingering for a moment before dropping her hand.

"If you'll let me, it'll soon follow your given name."

"Mia Collins-Hunter. It has a nice ring to it. Would you be Colton Hunter-Collins, too?"

"If you agree to be mine, I'll be anything you want me to be."

"Baby, I've already agreed to be yours. I love you," she tells me.

"I love you, Mia." I pull her towards me, kissing her slowly at first before my need rises and we get lost in the moment. With this perfect kiss, she makes me forget we're in a public place. I break our connection, cupping her face in my hands. I stare into her beautiful eyes, wondering how I got so damn lucky.

"You are so precious to me." I kiss her lips once again, then her nose and finally her forehead. "Mia, everything is better with you."

Epilogue

COLTON

I place my hand on Mia's knee to stop it from bouncing. "Babe, calm down."

"You say it like I want to be nervous! I have no choice."

"Yeah you do, it's just dinner."

"It's just dinner he says," she mocks me, and I can't help but smile.

"It is, babe."

"It's dinner at your dad's place."

"Yeah, and?" I ask pulling into my father's driveway. For the first time in a while I'm happy to be home. Happy to spend time with my family, and happy to have my girl right here with me.

"They're the most important people in your life," she practically yells as I turn off the car.

"You've met them before."

"Yes, but not all at the same time. And not as—"

"As the most important person in my life?" I ask, quoting her earlier words while staring at my beautiful girlfriend. Girlfriend doesn't seem like an adequate word to describe her. She's more like my partner, and I'm so lucky to have her. So lucky that she decided to give me a chance because even though I didn't lay a hand on Abbigail, I'm still not worthy of Mia.

I don't think I'll ever be, but that won't stop me from trying to be good enough for her every day until I don't have any days left.

"No, as your girlfriend meeting the most important people in your life," she says and I catch her hand before she swats me on the shoulder.

"Babe, they know. You've met my dad, and he thinks you're good for me. You've met Nick, and I'm sure if it weren't because you're mine and he knows I'd kill him, he'd be trying to put the moves on you," I say, bringing my lips to her hand and placing a kiss there. "And Kaitlyn, well, if she didn't like you, she wouldn't have begged you to take me back," I tell her trying to calm her nerves. She doesn't really know what's waiting for her when she gets inside.

"You promise it'll be okay?" she asks, and I see the vulnerability in her eyes. I know how important family is for her. Family is everything for this gorgeous girl sitting next to me. The one that believed she could do it all alone, but when her father came knocking, she opened herself up for a tentative relationship with him too. She's since met her little sister, and even the new woman in her father's life.

This girl's heart is so big no wonder she's made room there for me.

"I promise you," I answer, kissing her forehead.

"Okay, let's do this," she says full of that determination I love. I exit the car and run over to her side.

"You know you don't have to open the door for me every time," she says. I don't respond. Instead I bring my lips to hers, giving her some strength while she gives me the same.

MIA

"Would you two please stop making out in dad's driveway and get inside. I'm hungry!" I break the kiss and see Nick watching us from the front door.

"Fuck off," Colton responds, bringing his lips to mine once more.

"Watch your mouth," Colton's father says, and I break the kiss immediately. William is standing behind Nick, his arm resting on his son's shoulder while he watches Colton with a gleam in his eyes. I can see the love he has for his son, and the pride he feels is palpable.

"We'll continue this later," Colton whispers in my ear, holding my hand as we head inside. We follow Nick and William and make our way to what I believe is the dining room.

"Happy Birthday!" Everyone yells at once, and I see the room is filled with balloons and decorations. There's even a giant cake sitting in the middle of the table.

I turn back and look at Colton, whose gorgeous smile makes me feel a thousand times happier. "How did you know?"

"I may owe Kiya a few favors."

Of course she told him. My roommate has been on team Colton since the beginning. I get on my tippy-toes, closing the distance between us to show him how grateful I am for this. For how much he cares about me and how he shows it. The last birthday I had was after Mom passed, and that one wasn't worthy of celebration.

"Okay, that's enough. Save it for the wedding night!" William says from across the room, and the butterflies I fought so hard against in the beginning start fluttering within me.

"Seriously, I call maid of honor!" Kaitlyn chimes in, smiling at me. We both know she'd have to fight Kiya for that role. I'm amazed at how much closer Kaitlyn and I have gotten. She distanced herself from Abbigail after she tried to screw over her brother and me. All that Kaitlyn needed was good friends, and she's found that in Kiya and me.

"Best man sitting over here!" Nick adds, pointing at himself.

"Can we get married tomorrow?" Colton asks. I roll my eyes. While we won't be getting married tomorrow, I know we've just begun and there's no doubt in my mind that in the future, this man and I will still be together.

"No," I tell him, chuckling. I can't believe this is the conversation we're having right now.

"Soon though. I'm only getting older and I need me some grandbabies!" Colton's father states, and everyone roars with laughter.

"Soon," Colton assures his dad and my heart melts.

I look around me not only at the decorations in the room but the people. The people I've met at different times, whom have had struggles to overcome. The people who could have been torn apart by life, but somehow were resilient and have remained together.

"Thank you all so much for this."

"You're family," Nick says.

"You're one of us," William says, echoing his son's sentiment.

"You already know Colton is going to make you Mrs. Hunter," Kaitlyn adds, making me smile.

"You're already a Hunter. You have been since the day I first laid eyes on you," Colton finishes and tears brim in my eyes because although we haven't known each other for long, I already feel like I'm a part of his life—a part of his family.

"I love you," I tell him.

"And I love you. I always will."

Author's Note

I started writing this book in January 2017 and stopped so many times. I thought it was never going to be finished. I decided to give it up and started writing something else. But a couple of months later, the characters started talking to me again. They wouldn't let me sleep, so I finally wrote Mia & Colton the story they wanted. I told myself, that even if no one liked it, I did and that's what mattered. So, I pushed myself and wrote as many words as I could until it was finished.

The main lesson I wanted this book to leave you with is that you need others to make you better. Better With You, to me, means that another person can lift you up and help you instead of put you down. We are no damsels in distress waiting for our knight in shining armor. The man of our dreams is allowed to have moments of weakness, and that's what I wanted you to see with M&C.

Mia and Colton make each other stronger, make each other better, and that's why I love them.

This book was also a way for me to give back. I met some wonderful girls while on Spring Break who changed my life. They were survivors of human sex trafficking, and they were as young as 5 years old. It broke my heart, and so I wanted to bring it up in this book. Those girls taught me so much, I wanted to give back in whatever way I could.

They made me want to do better. Want to be better.

Other Titles by Gianna Gabriela

Bragan University Series

Better With You (Book #1)
Fighting For You (Book #2)
Falling for You (Book #3)
Better With You, Always (Book #4)

COMING SOON

Waiting For You (Book #5)
Finally With You (Book #6)

Not Alone Novellas

Not the End (Book #1)
Not the Same (Book #2)

COMING SOON

Not Alone (Book #3)

About Author
Gianna Gabriela

Gianna Gabriela is originally from Rhode Island. She's a small-town girl living in the Big Ol' City of New York. She considers herself a writer of gorgeous alpha-males and strong heroines. She's been reading for years and calls it her addiction. Her favorite genre is anything in the YA/NA Romance Realm.

She loves the saying that "a room without books is like a body without a soul." Her favorite color is black, she loves most sports, and doesn't like painting her nails because it takes a lot of work to remove the nail polish.

Follow me

Made in the USA
Columbia, SC
06 August 2019